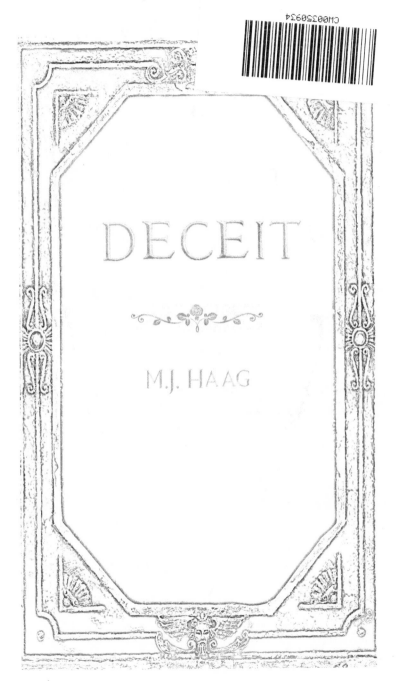

DECEIT

M.J. HAAG

ISBN 978-0-988852-38-9 (eBook Edition)
ISBN 978-1-943051-11-3 (Paperback Edition)
ISBN 978-1-515046-92-9 (CreateSpace Paperback Edition)

The characters and events in this book are fictitious. Any similar to real
persons, living or dead, is coincidental and not intended by the author.

Editing by Ulva Eldridge
Cover design by Shattered Glass Publishing LLC

To potato chips, late night reading,
and staying up until the alarm goes off.
Job well done.

CHAPTER ONE

Bryn's muffled sniffles faded as I stepped into the mists. I didn't go far before I hesitated. I could see the hand I held before me but nothing beyond that. Yet, visibility wasn't why I'd stopped. Fear held me in place.

The beast had always kept everyone at bay. Why had that changed? And, why with me? Knowing why he'd gone to such lengths to trap me within the estate might have assured me. Then again, perhaps his reasons were something to fear.

The beast's tail thumped against my stomach, a reminder of the bargain I'd made. To save my father, I had no choice but to clasp the tail and allow him to lead me through the mist. Walking away from my family was difficult, but walking toward my unknown future was harder.

Instead of leading me to the overgrown yard just

outside of the kitchen, he turned slightly east. It wasn't long before gravel crunched under my feet. I frowned at the sound and at the sudden disappearance of his tail.

"Go where you wish within the boundaries of the estate. Do as you please, with the exception of leaving," he said, as he moved behind me.

The mist retreated with him and revealed a grand entrance to the manor that he so zealously protected. Three steps laid with large slabs of natural grey stone led up to a sheltered court. Great columns of the same stone supported a roof to protect guests who might arrive during inclement weather.

The claw-ravaged, large double doors stood open in invitation. Yet, instead of welcome, their gaping maw conveyed an eerie sense of desolation. With reluctance, I climbed the steps and entered the beast's home.

For the first time, I saw the interior of the manor clearly. Aged décor, perfectly preserved from the ravages of time, yet marred by the beast's anger and negligence, drew my curious gaze. Did he truly only need a maid?

"Should I clean, then?" I asked, knowing he still lingered behind me.

"Do as you please," he said irritably.

Taking him at his word, I went from room to room, studying the place I would now call home. Though I did not care for cleaning, a good straightening would make it a fair place to live. As I wandered, I took time to right a tumbled chair or straighten thrown papers. In some places, shards of broken objects dusted the floor, and I made note to come back with a broom as my boots crunched over them.

I lost count of the turns and rooms I visited while the beast trailed me, cloaked in his now small cloud of mist. Other than the library, I noted nothing of particular interest until I reached the second floor.

In the midst of the beast's destruction, a single room remained untouched, and I didn't blame him for avoiding it. Frills, perfumes, and pillows filled the room with their noxious pink shades. I had no issue with pink in small doses. However, what lay before me made my eyes hurt. The only exception to the overabundance, a set of black, glossy doors, called to me.

They were set into the interior wall to the side and begged for the beast's angry furrows. Yet, none decorated the surface.

I crossed the pink rugs and opened the door. On the other side, the wood bore the worst marks I'd witnessed, gouging so deep only a thin layer of wood prevented a hole. I gently ran my fingers over the marks, staring at the torn grains.

As I watched, a piece smaller than a hangnail twitched, slowly straightening itself to mend the gash. I would have watched longer, fascinated by the display of enchantment, but the mess inside the room distracted me. Everything from the mattress and bed hangings to the inlaid wood patterns of the floor had been shredded.

"My room," he said from behind me. "This room is yours."

I turned to look over my shoulder at the pink abomination.

"I'd rather we trade," I said under my breath.

I closed the doors and continued with my tour. For a while, I became hopelessly lost until I came to a hallway I recognized. It would take me a long while to learn the layout of his home. My home, I corrected myself.

Making my way toward the library, I decided to spend my day cleaning it, so I could turn it into my sanctuary. I wasn't sure what I would find. The day I'd read to him, I'd only caught a glimpse of it in the candle light. Today wasn't much different.

When I walked into the room, the curtains still covered the windows, making it hard to see even without his mist clouding the area. I found my way to the closest window and tugged the drapes wide open. Light poured in, and I turned to view the room. A small gasp escaped me at the vastness.

The large room boasted enough furniture for several sitting areas, though everything was knocked about haphazardly. Filled bookcases lined every wall, even above the two doors. The only interruptions were the four windows on the outer wall and a fireplace near the door from which I'd entered. Eager to see more, I moved to tug open each curtain and finally saw the library in full.

Ignoring the beast, I set to work righting furniture and

shoving pieces across the wood floor to the positions I wanted. Whenever I found a book tumbled to the floor, I set it on the small writing desk near the center window. Until I had a chance to discover how the books were categorized and ordered, I didn't want to place anything onto the shelves.

I worked for hours until the sudden whoosh of the fire lighting itself distracted me. A tray of food rested on a table I'd placed near the first seating arrangement. Wiping my dusty hands on my skirt, I went to sit and eat while my eyes drifted over the room, seeking what I would work on next. The area near where I sat was restored to order. The far side of the room still needed much attention.

After devouring every bite of fruit and cheese, I went back to work. By the time the sun set, the library met my approval, and I began to study the books. I counted twenty-two floor to ceiling segmented bookcases. In each, there were at least fifteen shelves. Most were organized by subject, then author. However, several shelves seemed to be dedicated to a particular author.

Slowly, I began to see where the fallen books I had collected belonged and started to tuck them back into place. One shelf in particular gave me trouble as it towered just out of my tiptoed reach. Looking down at the lower shelf, I wondered if it would support my weight.

Rising to two legs, the beast stepped up behind me, plucked the book from my grasp, and then easily slid it into its place. Startled, I stared at his furred arm until it disappeared from view, not daring to turn around.

"Do not climb on the shelves," he said, having guessed my intent. "You will fall."

As quickly as he'd crowded me, I felt him move away; and I released the breath I'd held. When I looked around the room, I noticed him in the furthest, darkest corner, his mist obscuring him. I'd been so engrossed in the library I'd forgotten his presence.

"Thank you," I said softly.

A clock in the corner chimed for the half hour. I glanced at the face, saw how late it was, and yawned.

"Come. Eat. I will take you to your room afterwards," the beast said from his corner.

Again a tray with fruits, nuts, and cold water waited for me on the table. I ate everything then followed him through the dim, lamplit hallways, memorizing the path from the library to my room.

He opened the door to the room and stood aside to let me enter. As I passed him, my arm brushed against his torso, and he growled. A shiver of fear ran through me.

"Good night," he said simply and left me alone in the profusely pink room.

Giving the room a more thorough inspection than I had the first time, I found the bed soft and inviting, the wardrobe full of clothes, and a soft cloth waiting by the bowl of warm water on the washstand. I wiped the dust from my face and hands then went to the wardrobe and found several nightgowns, all sheer, with matching sheer wraps. At least they weren't pink, I thought as I undressed and slipped into a pale blue one.

I climbed into bed and thought of my family. I didn't doubt that the beast had freed them; he wanted me here willingly, for whatever his reasons. By now, I imagined my family had returned safely to the Water. Curling onto my side, I wondered how they would fare without me. Though I hoped that having one less mouth to feed would ease some of Father's burden, I knew he would rather have me home than here. Yet, the beast's manor didn't seem too terrible. I was free to roam inside the manor, regularly fed, and, so far, no demands had been made of me.

Sighing, I closed my eyes and wondered what I would do to occupy myself here. As interesting as this enchanted place was, if the rest of my days followed today, I would grow bored quickly.

THE NEXT MORNING, I rose late and reluctantly slipped from my warm bed—Father's mattress could not compare to the one I now called my own. Fresh, warm water again waited on the washstand for me to wash my face. I enjoyed not having to walk outside to fetch my own. However, when I turned to dress, I frowned in confusion at the empty chair beside the wardrobe. I was certain I'd draped my only dress there when I'd prepared for bed the night before.

I opened the wardrobe, thinking it had been magically placed in there while I slept. Inside, luxurious diaphanous gowns waited, a pale rainbow of colored skirts. No doubt, my dress had disappeared so I would wear one of his choosing. Sighing, I picked one at random. At least I had clothes. It could be worse, I thought, recalling his wish to see me when I'd bathed. He might have decided to have me walk about naked as the sisters did. I only wished I understood his purpose in having me here and dressing me in such a fashion.

The pale green dress I chose slipped over my head easily. The layered skirts afforded a shadowy glimpse at my legs. The bodice flattened my small breasts, making every detail clearly visible. Chewing my lip, I debated how to preserve some of my modesty. My eyes drifted to the wraps that I'd deemed worthless for cover.

I tore off both sleeves of the matching wrap and folded them in half to tuck the additional two layers of material into my bodice. It had the desired effect of blotting out the details while giving just a hint of what the bodice hid. I stepped into the flimsy slippers that matched the gown and left my room with the intent to spend the day reading.

In the library, a breakfast tray waited, but I ignored it to walk to the writing desk and retrieved the book on farming I'd set aside. It was the one I'd started reading to the beast, and I wanted to read to its conclusion. I settled on the sofa near the tray and absently popped a bite of chilled, cooked meat into my mouth as I found my place.

"Did you sleep well?" the beast asked softly.

My insides jumped from the start he gave me, but I only nodded to answer him and kept my eyes on the page. After a few minutes of silence, I calmed enough to eat and again lost myself in the book.

"Did you find the clothes to your satisfaction?"

"Not quite," I said. "I fear going outside will give me a chill and be the death of me. I hope in winter I'll have something with a bit more substance."

He snorted but made no comment.

Well after eating my last bite, I finished the book and closed it with a snap. Intrigued by the problems farmers faced and the solutions posed by the author, I wandered to the shelf on farming, replaced the book, and selected another thin volume, which I brought back to the sofa.

"You like farming?" the beast asked with a note of uncertainty.

"Not really. But I like eating, and the two are definitely related."

He made no response, and I settled in to absorb the new author's thoughts. On one topic they both agreed. Repeated plantings resulted in poorer harvests. However, their solutions varied. One suggested letting the field lay fallow for several years. The other suggested the annual slaughtering be done over the field to slow the soil depletion. I didn't like the idea of eating carrots soaked in year old animal blood. I sought out another's opinion and kept searching through the volumes until I had almost twenty books on farming lying on the table next to the tray. I referenced from one to another until I came to a conclusion based on several tried methods.

"Fish and certain animal waste," I murmured, thumbing through several pages. "Perhaps vegetation, too. Interesting." I wished I had a way to ask Mr. Kinlyn how he prevented soil depletion.

I turned my gaze to the writing desk. The thought of writing Mr. Kinlyn led to the thought of writing Father.

"May I write letters and have them delivered?" I asked the beast.

"You may write, but I will read your correspondence before sending it," he said.

I stood and moved to the writing desk. Outside the window, I caught the movement of the female nymph, kneeling before her no longer solid partner. Before I could fully stop to wonder what they did, the beast rumbled a quick promise to return shortly and left the room.

Worried for the nymph, I rushed to the window and tossed it open. Both nymphs froze at the noise.

"He comes," I quickly whispered in warning. Both solidified at the sound of my voice.

As the dark mists roiled into view from the left, I noticed where the pair remained joined and blushed deeply. Apparently, the baker wasn't the only one who liked to taste.

Leaning further out the window, I called to the beast, concerned about his temper should he find his nymph solidified.

"Sir, do all the trees on the estate grow so peculiarly?"

He slowed at the sound of my voice and growled menacingly but did not approach the trees. Instead, he came to the window, bringing me close to his height as he stood on two legs. Through the mist, I saw one of his ears flick in agitation.

"Why did you open the window?"

"To get a better view of the beauty outside," I said calmly. "I didn't mean to disturb your time away from me. I will look at the trees later. They bear studying." I kept the insincerity from my voice.

With a last look at the trees, I closed the window and moved back to the sofa.

Another tray waited for me. Anxiously, I nibbled at the food, only tasting it when the beast returned. On the pretext of writing a letter, I passed the window and saw, to my joy, the pair unmarred.

The beast rejected my first few attempts at a letter to my father. The version he finally accepted included very little detail, only that I had enjoyed a day reading about farming and my findings on the subject. In closing, I wished Father well and promised to see him soon. Similarly, I penned a letter to Mr. Kinlyn to ask what treatments he gave his fields at the end of each season.

The crow I'd noticed in Konrall came to the window

when the beast called and took the letters in his beak before flying off again.

The afternoon faded to evening, and bored with the atmosphere of the library, I ambled through the house, the beast not far behind me. When I came to my room by chance, I decided to go to bed early and bade him good night. He growled and grumped but left me alone.

That night, the sound of my door opening roused me from my sleep enough that I lifted my head.

"Sleep, Benella," the beast whispered.

The bed dipped as he lay next to me and threaded his fingers in my hair. I slept.

A HOT BATH waited in my room when I woke. Naturally hesitant after my last experience bathing in the beast's lair, I stared at it before stripping. I couldn't avoid bathing forever and bathing once a week when I left this place didn't appeal to me, either.

Sinking into the warm water, I sighed but didn't waste time relaxing. After washing with an overly sweet smelling soap, I stepped from the water and wrapped a large towel around myself before opening the wardrobe. A lone garment waited within, a single panel of fabric which would leave nothing to the imagination. Turning to look for my nightgown, I noted that too had disappeared. I wrinkled my nose in frustration, until the garish pink curtains on the windows caught my eye.

When I stepped out into the hall, I wasn't surprised to see the beast waited. Ripped patches of pink discreetly hid my important parts, one long rectangle over my breasts and another uniquely shaped piece I'd tied at my sides to cover my backside and front.

The beast growled at the sight of me. I walked up to him, pressing through his mist until I saw his eyes inches from mine. He stood on all fours.

"Do you want me to fear you?" I asked, my breath moving his fur as I spoke.

He blinked at me.

"No."

"Then why do you keep growling at me? A growl in the animal world is meant as a warning and to inspire caution if not fear."

"I'm not an animal," he said with a growl still in his throat.

"Then stop acting like one," I said with a soft calm.

He blinked at me again then narrowed his eyes.

"I don't like your dress," he said.

"Much better," I said with a smile and reached out to pat his head. I knew I took a risk to treat him so; but if he insisted on playing games with me, I would play them back.

His eyes rounded at my touch, and I wondered if he'd growl again. Instead, he just watched me closely as I gave

M.J. HAAG

his head a final pat and turned away, not responding to his comment.

"May I have eggs for breakfast?" I asked pleasantly. "Oh, and bacon?" My mouth watered at the idea.

He answered with subdued approval and followed me through the hallways until I found the library. A tray already waited with the food I'd requested. Instead of searching for a book, I sat on the sofa and took a large bite.

"Do you eat?" I asked.

He'd pulled the mist around himself again, but not so fully that I couldn't see the outline of him.

"Of course," he answered.

"No need to sound so offended. Nothing else here seems normal, and you never eat with me, so I wasn't sure." I took several more bites. "What shall I do today?" I asked.

"Whatever you wish," he answered.

Finishing my meal, I found my way to the kitchen and wandered out the door. Every time I'd left the kitchen, I'd gone straight toward the estate's gates. This time, I turned left, hopefully toward the side of the manor with the library.

The dainty slippers did little to protect my feet as I tromped along, and my soles grew tender as I walked. Still, I pressed on until I walked the length of the front of the manor. Stopping, I looked up at one spot and counted four stories. Somehow, I'd missed seeing a staircase on the second story.

Rounding the corner, a patch of thick briars forced me away from the manor and into the woods. I felt a snag on my dress a moment before I heard the material rip. A good portion of my thigh was now exposed.

"I don't care for my dress either," I said over my shoulder in response to the beast's earlier comment.

He said nothing as he followed me.

By the time I circled around the briars, I sported several snags and tears in the dress and truly appreciated the pieces of curtain I'd tucked inside of it. I bled from a few small scrapes, but it was nothing that slowed me down.

Finally, I came to the place where I'd spotted the nymphs, but neither remained. Disappointed, I looked toward the window. It would have been a much shorter journey to have climbed out from there. Shaking my head, I continued in the same direction and eventually found the door the beast had used to reach the nymphs the day I'd read to him.

With relief, I limped back to the library and sat on the sofa to tug off my slippers. This wouldn't have happened if he had let me keep my boots. The cuts were starting to sting.

"I need better clothes," I said. "Sturdy ones that will stand up to briars and stones."

"No. If I cannot touch you, I will at least look at you."

"That's why I have to wear this? Fine." I flopped back

onto the sofa and put my feet up. "Touch my hair then give me boots, sturdy trousers, and a man's shirt."

A slight choked noise came from behind me, and I closed my eyes, not believing I'd let my temper escape.

"My apologies," he said. "Allow me to heal your injuries." It came as a demand rather than a request.

"I'd rather have trousers."

"Allow me to heal your injuries, and you will have your trousers when you journey outside."

"Fine," I said, knowing he'd neither offered boots nor a shirt. Trousers were a start, though.

His tongue lapped at my ankle, startling me from my thoughts. He moved higher, not needing to move the dress to soothe the cut on my knee. Warmth flooded me after his tongue found the light scrape on my thigh.

When he moved to the slight tear in the material on my stomach, I trembled, no longer certain of our deal. He ran his tongue over the tiny wound several times before moving upward. Then, he paused. His massive head hovered just above my breasts, the heat of his breath warming them.

Before I could think to panic, he continued upward toward my chin, and I recalled a branch that had snapped back at my face. The touch of his tongue so close to my mouth sent a shiver chasing through me. He licked me from just below my chin to my bottom lip.

"Touch me," he said.

My eyelids popped open, and I found myself staring

into his eyes. Large, wide set in his shaggy head and deep blue, they held me in place with no mist separating us. I raised a hand and gently placed it against his neck, the soft fur warming my fingers. Underneath, I felt him shudder, and I wondered how often he felt anyone's touch. Probably never. The creatures here seemed to fear him as much as the townspeople.

"Tell me true, did I miss any?" he whispered.

Reluctantly, I nodded and rolled to my stomach, breaking our contact.

He laved the scrapes on the backs of my legs and arms and then the bottoms of my feet, which made me twitch and giggle involuntarily. When he finished, he moved away from me, retreating into the mist.

For the rest of the day, I contented myself with books and tried to forget his presence.

No TROUSERS WAITED in the wardrobe the next day, just a selection of translucent gowns. Smiling at the selection, I picked the most modest dress from them and tucked another ripped panel from the curtains, which hadn't disappeared.

The beast waited in the hallway with less mist than the day before.

"I don't like the dress," he said again.

"Me neither," I said agreeably. "I thought I would be able to wear trousers today."

"If you would like to go out again today, you can change in the servant's quarters in the kitchen. Your trousers are there and are only meant for outside. Inside, I want you wearing the dresses you find within your wardrobe."

Nodding, I walked hurriedly toward the kitchen. True to his word, trousers waited on one of the beds as did boots and a cream shirt. I quickly closed the door and changed. The trousers were a bit snugger than I was used to, as was the shirt, but the boots fit well.

Eagerly, I stepped from the room and held out my arms to do a slow turn for the beast.

"Well?" I prompted with a smile on my face.

"Lovely," he said.

Happy with the clothes, I led the way out the door. As I slowly explored the area in front of the manor, the beast paced behind me. Near lunch, I sensed his growing impatience and knew my time outside would soon come to an end. It didn't upset me. It had been an enjoyable outing.

"Go change," he said. "Do not wear these clothes inside unless you want to lose them."

I went back into the servant's quarters and closed myself in to change. Immediately, I saw what he'd done. The dress remained where I'd set it, but my scraps of curtain were missing. I sat heavily on the mattress, its material too thick to tear without the help of a knife. There was nothing else to shield myself from his gaze. If I stayed in the trousers or tried to use the shirt in some way, I had no doubt they would be gone in the morning, and I would not see them again.

Defeated for the moment, I put on the dress and marched out the door. The table in the kitchen was laden with food.

"I'm not hungry," I said and turned to leave.

"Stop. Turn and show me your dress as you did when you changed this morning."

Teeth clenched to keep from telling him what I thought of him, I slowly turned a circle, keeping my arms at my side.

"If you're finished demeaning me, I'd like to go to my room."

He growled low and long.

"Sit. Eat. Or I will feed you."

Glaring at the swirling mist near the door of the kitchen, I marched to the table, spotted a bowl filled with meat and gravy, and stuck my hand in it. Pulling a fist full of dripping meat from it, I proceeded to shove it in my mouth in the most grotesque, unladylike fashion I could imagine.

His roar shook the windows, but I ignored him, swallowed the lump of meat, and reached for the roasted baby potatoes. With my hand. I crammed one in my mouth and chewed noisily.

"I said sit."

I sat heavily on the chair, not bothering to face the table. Never taking my eyes from him, I reached to the side and grabbed the next item. Stewed plums. Though a disgusting dish I usually avoided, I didn't blink as I shoved some in my mouth and dribbled juice down the front of my dress. The plums gagged me when I swallowed, and I lost the remaining threads of my temper.

Without standing, I grabbed the dish and threw it with all my might at the beast, whose form briefly appeared in the mist. The bowl hit him squarely, broke apart, and drenched him in the sugared plum sauce.

The mist disappeared, and I saw the rage in his eyes.

"Run," he whispered.

A shiver ran through me, and I bolted from my chair, my skirt floating around my legs as I ran for my room. I wouldn't make it unless he chose to let me.

Behind me, I heard a mighty crash and another roar.

He didn't sound like he was in the mood to let me escape.

My slippered feet slid on the wood floor as I changed direction to turn down the first hall I found. I kept running and turning until I was in the library. Shoving the window wide, I leapt out and landed on my feet, startling the nymphs who were back at it.

"Run," I whispered to them.

Inside, the beast roared. The male ran, but the female hesitated.

"Go!" I urged her as I turned toward the back of the

manor. The female hooked my arm and turned me toward the east, giving me a little shove. I ran.

The beast's cries faded as I put distance between us. A stitch in my side grew to a cramp when I finally burst through the trees and fell face first into a familiar pool. I rolled onto my back and came up sputtering in knee-deep water.

After wiping my eyes, I tried to silence the harsh gasp of my breaths so I might listen for the beast. In the distance, I heard him calling my name.

"Child," a voice grated nearby.

I turned to look at the old tree, the face already formed.

"He will learn. Do not give up. Do not run."

The tree untwisted, closing its mouth and eyes just before the beast burst upon the clearing. My eyes widened at the sight of him as he stood at the pond's edge, breathing harshly and fully visible on all fours. His raised hackles and bared teeth sent a shiver of fear though me, as did the low crackling growl emanating from him. The tree wanted me to stay. I desperately wanted to run.

Trembling with fear and cold, I did what the tree suggested and stood my ground.

"Will you hurt me now?" The words barely escaped my tight throat. Yet, I knew he heard them for his growl deepened. Despite his anger, he remained on the bank.

I gripped my heavy skirts and exhaled slowly. Then, with my shoulders back, I bravely walked toward him. My heart thrummed in my chest. Certainly he could hear it; I could hear little else.

As I approached, his growl softened while the fur on his neck continued to stand up harshly. He glared at me as I stood before him. I cautiously reached out and smoothed his fur down.

He didn't move away. Instead, I felt the flesh under my palm quiver. The beast's gaze met mine, and I saw the storm there. The undeniable rage was still present, but I also saw sadness and frustration. My heart went out to the tortured creature, and I cautiously embraced him.

When I leaned my head against his neck, all noise stopped. Not just his growl, but the animated chirping of the birds, the rustling of the leaves, everything.

Plum sauce matted his hair.

"The plums were too disgusting to throw at you," I whispered. "I should have thrown the potatoes, instead."

I watched his hackles slowly relax.

"Why did you not want to eat?" he finally asked.

I snorted.

"It wasn't the food that bothered me. It's the clothes. I don't like pink, and I don't like dresses. When you run, they trip you; and I like to run. And I don't like being treated like a whore."

His teeth ground together.

"I do not treat you like a whore."

"How is making me wear these dresses so you can see

22

all my personal parts not treating me like a whore?" I asked, keeping my head resting against his neck.

His hackles started to rise again, so I reached up and smoothed them down. He grunted in response and seemed to calm. I didn't touch him more than necessary, cautious of the sisters' lesson.

"Come," he said instead of answering me. "You will catch a chill if we stay here longer."

I moved away from him so he could lead. I didn't miss the long look he gave my wet, clinging dress. Biting my tongue to keep from whispering the word whore, I patted the tree as I passed, thankful for its advice.

IN MY ROOM, another bath waited along with a tray of food and a note that simply said *No plums*.

Smiling, I ate the food then peeled myself out of the clingy, damp dress. The plum juices had stained it, ruining the material. I felt no remorse as I dropped it to the floor.

CHAPTER TWO

On the fifth day, the wardrobe remained empty. I scowled at it and whispered a single word. "Beast." And I meant his nature, not his name.

After the fight in the kitchen, I had thought he'd understood and would relent. Still he had insisted on the sheer clothes. Yesterday when I had woken, the curtains had vanished; and I'd torn a patch from my bedding to cover myself.

Now, I tugged a whole blanket from my bed to wrap around my shoulders before stomping to the hallway. Today was the day I was supposed to go see my father. I'd gone to bed early, so I could rise before first light, not wanting to waste any of the time I could spend with my family.

In the hall, the beast waited as usual.

"Why do I have no clothes?" I asked.

"Are you visiting your father today?" he asked much too calmly.

"Yes, I wanted to." His calm just upset me more.

"Then the dresses you have wouldn't suit. You can wear your trousers, which are in the kitchen."

The annoyance left me. Of course I couldn't wear the clothes he chose to town. I had assumed he wouldn't think of that on his own.

"Thank you," I said, turning to race to the kitchen.

He snagged the blanket, stopping my departure.

"Leave this here."

Normally, once I found a way to cover myself, he didn't order it away. Surprised, I glanced back at him.

"Now."

I averted my gaze and let the blanket fall to the floor. When I started to walk away from him, I wondered if he found the view of my backside as mesmerizing as Ila's had been that first time I'd seen it. The thought of Ila made me smile. I couldn't wait to see my friends again and wondered what Father had told them about my absence. I hurried my pace until I ran, eager to start my journey.

In the kitchen, I closed myself in the servant's quarters to change. As soon as I opened the door of the servant's quarters, the beast gave me a warning.

"We bargained one day a week. I grant that you may leave the gates after the sun rises and must return to them before the sun sets. Do not be late or I will fetch your father in recompense."

Nodding jerkily, I left him in the kitchen and raced toward the gate as the sky lightened. From the corner of my eye, I spotted one of the nymphs but it solidified before I could see which.

The gates swung open for me as the beast called my name. I stopped just inside the iron barrier.

The beast appeared beside me, his breath as heavy as mine.

"Will you return?" he asked gruffly.

In that question, I glimpsed his uncertainty of me. I didn't understand why he wanted me to stay. But, I understood that whatever his reasons, I mattered to him; and he worried that the fear for my father's safety wasn't enough to bring me back. Feeling a small measure of pity for him, I nodded again before walking out the gate.

Freedom flavored the air with a sweetness that I inhaled deeply as I alternated between walking and jogging. When I came in sight of the bridge, a crow that was roosted on one of the bridge supports shook the spray from his feathers and took flight, spiraling high over the Water. I didn't stop to see if it flew toward the estate.

With a light step, I walked through the market district, smiling at the early merchants as I made my way toward my father's house. At the Sisters' house, I caught a glimpse of someone and paused to wave up at the windows. Then, I continued on. When I stood before Father's small home, I paused for a moment and wistfully watched the smoke curling from the chimney. I had missed them all so much.

Without knocking, I pushed the door open, a smile on my lips. As I suspected, Bryn stood at the stove cooking something. She looked up at me, her eyes wide with surprise.

"Benella," she said, clearly surprised by my arrival. Her gaze touched my face then my clothes before clouding with disapproval. "You look fit and well fed. I hope you're not expecting to eat; there's not enough."

Her attitude did nothing to curb my joy in seeing her. I stepped in and closed the door behind me.

"How are you, Bryn? What happened after I last saw you?" I really wanted to know about the possibility of her being pregnant.

"We left the estate and walked to Konrall. Father still hoped to sell a book. He warned us not to speak of you or the estate." She turned away from me and poked at the meat sizzling in the pan. "He asked me if I would be happy in a forced marriage with Tennen. I said I would not; and we haven't spoken of anything, except you, since then."

"Me?" How could Father not ask questions of the baby? Obviously he'd deduced that Tennen had fathered it, but didn't he want to know how long ago? And, there were other questions that needed answers. How much time remained until the baby arrived? Did Bryn have other prospects? Had she felt the babe move yet?

"Of course, you. The beast took you. We all worried, thinking you wouldn't return to us. We should have known better," she said bitterly. Before I could respond, she continued. "Did you bring anything back with you? Things are not much better than they were those few days ago."

"I'm sorry. I did not." I hadn't thought of anything other than seeing them again. The next visit I would be better prepared.

The door burst open just then, and Father rushed in. He spun me about and caught me up in a tight hug. Finally, the welcome I'd hoped for. I wrapped my arms around him in return, smelling the faint tang of the sisters' incense.

"Father," Bryn said in surprise. "What are you doing home?"

"Someone told me they saw Benella," he said as he pulled back from me. A smile lined his mouth, but his eyes looked sadder than usual.

"But your work. Shouldn't you—"

"My employer has a fond spot for Benella and granted me time to spend with her this afternoon." Father dropped his arms from around me. "Benella, walk with me. Bryn, we will return for lunch." He turned and walked out the door.

When I looked at Bryn, I saw tears in her eyes.

"It'll be okay, Bryn. I'll be back later and want to hear what names you've picked so far for the baby." Her eyes widened, but then she offered me a small, sad smile.

I caught up with Father and wrapped my hand around his arm.

"Why are you angry with Bryn?" I asked.

"Her dalliance will cost her, robbing her of a marriage to a decent man."

Pulling back on his arm slightly, I stopped us in the street and turned him to look at me.

"Her dalliance will rob her of nothing because a decent man will look at her and see her worth and welcome the child she carries. The ones who won't see her worth or shun her because of the baby are not decent."

Father shook his head, but smiled at me indulgently.

"If only she had your sense of responsibility," he said.

"Father, how can you say that? Bryn has been responsible for all of us since Mother died. She's taken on so much responsibility so early it's a wonder her shoulders aren't curved from it. Despite that responsibility, she's still young and prone to a young woman's fancy. Tennen looked at her sweetly and played on her hopes. Don't fault her for her naivety of a man's character."

During my speech, my father's mouth dropped a bit. I probably sounded pompous.

"And don't hold me in too harsh a light when I make my own naïve mistakes."

"Wise beyond your years," he muttered, and we started walking again. "So what would you have me do?"

"Can't you see how frightened she is? She's probably wondering where she will be by the time the babe is born. Reassure her that you still love her and care. Ask about baby names or see if Blye has given her any tiny garments.

I will try to find some way to help, too, the next time I return."

"You are not here to stay?"

I shook my head.

"He will allow me to visit you once a week. But I must have care to return before my allotted time."

He sighed and looked at me with concern.

"Just take care of yourself." We neared the Sister's back door. "I will want details when we eat lunch together."

I nodded and followed him in. He frowned at me slightly but made no comment when Ila waited with a cup of tea for me.

Ila remained quiet until Father walked away.

"We've missed you. Your father wouldn't say where you'd gone, even though Aryana pestered him constantly."

She led the way to the bathing chambers where Aryana lounged in one of the tubs.

"Benella," she spoke in soft delight. "I'm so happy to see you. Tell us where you've been."

I smiled as she stepped from the water and followed us to the back room. It felt like a ritual to bathe as soon as I came to the Sisters' house, and I wondered if this is how the men felt when they arrived.

"Employed," I said vaguely as Gen left the room. "Father came here because of me, so I wanted to repay his care of me. I'm granted one day in seven to return to visit." I let them undress me as I continued in a concerned whisper. "How has he been?"

"Distracted," Aryana answered as she set my clothes aside. She turned back to me and tilted her head in study. "You look like you gained some weight back."

I felt a blush creep into my skin, and she laughed huskily.

"Tell me about your new master," she said. "Does he treat you well?"

"He's confusing," I admitted. "And prickly. I think he's so used to everyone bending to his will, he doesn't know how to react when I start questioning him."

Ila poured water over me, and Aryana gave a small smile as she picked up the soap.

"Why do you question him?" she asked.

I laughed.

"Why does anyone question? To learn. All my life I have lived under the roof of a man I knew and understood. Now I find myself guessing and stumbling around in the dark. It's uncomfortable not being able to anticipate the direction of his thoughts. I've spent the last several days focused on his library. It's a lovely, large room filled with so many books. When I'd started, it had been a mess. Does he think I restored the room properly? Are the books in the correct order? Should I clean the adjoining room next or move to another wing entirely? When I start asking questions, I get irritable replies as if I'm bothering him."

I realized I'd started to raise my voice, so I took a calming breath again.

Aryana's hands soothed the muscles in my back while I

tried to ignore Ila's hands washing my front. Ila's smirk told me she knew it, too.

"I am grateful that I'm no longer a burden on Father, but do wonder why my employer even wanted me there if he can't be bothered to give me direction."

"You are on the right path," Aryana murmured. "Ask questions; study him. You will learn."

Ila handed me the soap so I could finish washing as she fetched the rinse water. Rinsed of the soap, I followed them to the tubs, again noting how they walked with such ease.

"I'm curious," I said hesitantly.

"Of course you are," Ila laughed. "If you weren't, you wouldn't be in this house."

Smiling, I nodded in agreement.

"How do you walk about with such confidence and no clothes?" I asked as we each settled into a tub.

"What about clothes gives you confidence?" Aryana asked.

"A sound question," I said as I thought it over. "I suppose it hides our faults."

Aryana stood suddenly and held out her arms.

"Do you see faults?"

"Well, I'm not a good judge," I said. "I've not seen many women naked."

Aryana sat with a laugh.

"I have, and I will tell you that the men who come here have a hard time finding flaws in limbs or torso. They only see a body and not the person associated with it. So, we wear a veil to hide the person in which they might find fault."

I continued to think over her answer in silence. Is that how the beast wanted to see me when I wore his dresses? As a body and not a person?

Too soon, she insisted we leave the waters and dress again.

I RAN the last several yards to the estate as the sun sank below the tree line. I was cutting it close. The gate grated open for me, and I flew through the gap without slowing and collided with the beast, who had been waiting in mist clouded shadows.

"Returned as promised," I panted as I took a step back from him and bent to rest my hands on my knees.

In response to my announcement, he turned so the tip of his tail brushed my face. With a grimace, I straightened, clasped his tail, and allowed him to lead me, even though I knew I could find my own way. The fur of his tail stood out stiffly, and I surmised my return so close to sunset had given him concern.

Though I didn't like his threats against my father, I did feel a measure of pity for the beast. I could only imagine how lonely his life was within the walls of the estate.

My stomach began growling before we reached the kitchen.

"Change," he ordered after we walked through the outer door.

The mist pulled back to the small area where he paced.

Sensing his barely contained mood, I slipped into the servant's quarters and gently closed the door. The nightgown I'd removed just that morning now lay on the first bed. With a sigh, I put it on and thought again of Aryana's logic.

I didn't want the beast to only see me as a body. I wanted him to see me as a person, faults and all. After all, we all had faults. Why put me in a position where I would disappoint him when he discovered I wasn't what he wanted? But what did he want?

Knowing it would anger him, but unwilling to bend, I put the shirt on over the gown, wearing it unbuttoned like a wrap. When I opened the door, he growled loudly but didn't order the shirt away.

"Sit and eat," he said.

On the table, there was another full meal similar to the one I'd thrown at him. This time, I sat gracefully and politely consumed what was before me. I ate until my stomach stretched with pain, then used my napkin to dab my mouth. With a content sigh, I rose.

"Thank you," I said.

"Why did you wear the shirt? I warned that you would lose it if you wore it inside," he said, still in a poor mood.

"The gown left me feeling exposed and cold," I said.

"Take it off."

I walked toward him without reaching for the shirt. The rasp of his pacing silenced as he stopped to watch me.

The mist still obscured everything but his outline. Walking through it, I stopped when only an inch separated us. The mist tried gathering, but I stood too close for it to shield him. Looking into his eyes, I calmly shed the shirt and draped it over my arm. Then, I tilted my head and studied his pointed, furred ears, his very sharp teeth exposed by his pulled back lips, and his deep set blue eyes shot red with anger.

"Staring at the beast?" he asked with his clicking growl.

"Staring at the Benella?" I asked curiously.

He huffed a great breath that moved the hair loosened from my braid.

"If you want me to bare myself to you, be prepared to bare yourself to me," I said.

He turned away, his claws scraping harshly against the stone floor of the kitchen.

"Do as you like," he said as he tore open the door. It slammed closed behind him.

I wrapped the shirt around me again and made my way to my bedroom. Without hesitating, I opened the double doors to his room and walked to his wardrobe. There, I selected a new shirt, much larger than my own, and shed my gown. If I were to lose a shirt I wore, I'd rather that shirt be his.

Securely wrapped in a man's fine shirt, I curled under my covers and wondered what the beast would think of the gown and shirt I'd left in his wardrobe. I drifted to sleep with a slight smile on my lips.

AFTER WASHING MY FACE, I went to the wardrobe and saw it filled with a variety of gossamer dresses once again. I closed the doors and opted to walk about the manor in his shirt to see what he had to say about it. Though it bared my legs from just above the knee, it covered me more thoroughly than any of the dresses would.

The beast waited in the hall, as usual, when I opened the door, his thick mist protecting him.

"Good morning. What shall we do today?"

"Do as you wish," he said softly.

His calm voice surprised me. I'd been prepared for another rant or argument.

"Do as I wish? Don't you grow bored following me around?" I asked, making my way toward the library, listening to his soft steps behind me.

"That's not your concern."

"What exactly are my concerns?"

"Staying within the walls," he said immediately.

"Unless it's my day to leave, correct?"

"Of course," he said, his voice rough with agitation.

I stopped walking and turned to face him. We stood in

the wide hallway just outside of the library. The mist acted as a wall separating us, but I saw him pace back and forth through it, backlit by a candle that quickly winked out.

"Do you intend to hurt me? Now or eventually?"

He snorted.

"No."

"You like watching me, no matter what I do; and after the month is up, you intend to touch me," I said as a statement of fact. "You've stated you do not want me to fear you. And you've kept me fed and sheltered. Yet through it all, I feel you growing angrier." I went on quickly before he could say anything. "Now, I admit, I've done several things —many, actually—to contribute to your ire. So I'm wondering if my presence is really providing you with any value. Undoubtedly, I am reaping more benefits than you. Why keep me?"

He growled, and I knew what he was about to say.

"I know," I sighed. "It is not my concern. But did you consider that if you shared the purpose of my presence with me, I might not be so difficult about what you request of me? That maybe I might understand your reasons and assist you as best I can in return for all the favor you've given me?"

Silence greeted my logic.

I turned and walked into the library, listening to the brush of his paws against the floor.

Not in the mood for anything particular, I browsed the shelves until a gilded book upon one of the highest shelves caught my eye. Tilting my head back, I stared at it. I had no hope of reaching it.

"Step onto my hand," the beast said from behind me.

I looked down and saw his furry paw extended forward.

"Won't I be too heavy to lift with one hand?"

He made a noise between a grunt and a laugh. I supposed he was very strong if he could throw grown men up and over the walls of the estate. I kicked off the delicate slipper and raised my foot, holding the shelf for balance.

"The other one, too," he said, offering his other hand.

I stood on his hands, and he easily lifted me as he shifted from the crouch in which he'd started to his full height. It brought me higher than the book. Placing a steadying hand on a shelf, I bent slightly to reach for it.

He lifted me higher, keeping the book just out of reach so I needed to bend lower. I rolled my eyes at his game and reached for the book again.

His tongue rasped the back of my thigh, and I froze.

"I changed my mind. I would like to get down."

"Not yet," he whispered, lifting me higher.

Still in his hands, I dropped to a squat and twisted to face him. I caught him with his tongue hanging out for the next swipe, and he licked my face instead of my thigh. We both looked at each other in surprise.

"You promised," I reminded him. "A month. You know this is a breach in our bargain."

"No more than the shirt."

I couldn't argue. He'd told me he wanted to at least see me if he couldn't touch me.

"What guarantee do I have you won't touch me if you do see me? I thought seeing a woman's body caused," I flapped a hand while my face grew warm. "Well, I thought it grew a man's desire to touch her. Wouldn't I just be putting myself in danger?"

"No," he said firmly. "If I see you, I wouldn't need to touch you. Only two days a week. The rest you could wear what you wish."

I narrowed my eyes at him. Why the change in our deal? Were we getting closer to the real reason for my presence?

"Please set me down. I need to consider this carefully."

He immediately set me on my own feet and followed me as I slowly moved to sit on the sofa. I remained quiet for several minutes, keeping my thoughts to myself, and he again began to pace in agitation.

Walking about without clothes might have seemed unsettling if not for my association with the Whispering Sisters. For them, it appeared completely natural and served a purpose. What purpose would my nudity serve, though, if not to entice as theirs did? I didn't know, and I didn't like not knowing.

There were several points in my life where I'd made decisions not based on logic or concern for my well-being, but simply based on curiosity. I knew this would be another instance. I wanted to discover his purpose. However, there were some concerns I couldn't put aside.

"I will agree, but I have a few conditions and some questions you must answer."

"No questions," he said with irritation.

"Come now, you don't even know what they are. How can you deny them? For instance, I've noticed several enchanted beings here. The wood nymphs, the crow. I'm sure there are others. I would like to know if you intend that they will see me naked."

He growled low, the click becoming so pronounced that it seemed the growl stopped and started in bursts.

"No one will see you but me," he said.

"See?" I smiled slightly. "Not such hard questions. May I choose the days?"

"Yes," he growled. His pacing grew more agitated.

"I'm not convinced I will be completely safe once we start this. If I should die at the estate, I want you to provide for my family."

He stopped pacing, and through the mist, I saw him turn toward me fully.

"You will not die." Then he added softly, "But I agree to your terms."

"Then one last thing," I said, taking a calming breath. He wouldn't like this condition, but I wouldn't sway from it. "No more mist. I need to trust that you will not harm me. I can't trust what you keep hidden from me."

"If you see me, you will trust me less."

Chewing my lip for a moment, I struggled to come up with a solution that would work for both of us.

"What if you gave me a few hours each day without the mist so I could know you better?"

He grunted his agreement, but the mist remained. I didn't mind. Trust took time.

"Go change," he said abruptly.

Or maybe time wasn't something the beast wanted to acknowledge. I stood reluctantly. I'd agreed to the terms. The only concern that remained was his treatment of me. Yet, even if something happened to me as a result of my folly, my father and sisters would benefit from it.

Without comment, he followed my slow progress through the halls until we reached my door.

"Pick what you like from the wardrobe. Your own this time," he said.

Clothes? I'd thought he'd meant me to run around naked.

I slipped into my room and rushed to pull open the wardrobe doors. Ruffled masses of pink horror filled the space. I made a face as I pulled one out. Blye would love to wear the dress I held. It laced up the front, and the layered skirt would cover all my important parts, so I couldn't complain.

Sighing, I let my shirt fall to the floor and tugged the dress over my head, lacing up the front. After sliding my feet into the matching slippers, I opened the door and turned for his inspection.

"I'd expected a happier face," he said with a puzzled note.

"I'm sorry, I'm just not used to wearing anything so...fancy." I had almost said feminine.

"That's the point. To provide you the things you couldn't have before."

"What if I liked the things I had before? Well, except the lack of food. I like the food here," I quickly added, hoping I'd get breakfast soon.

"If you could wear anything you wished," he asked slowly, "what would you wear?"

I grinned and answered promptly.

"Trousers and a sturdy shirt."

"Even indoors?" he asked.

I nodded and wondered what he thought of my preference. He didn't leave me waiting long.

"I would prefer you wear dresses, and in the future, I will offer you options that you might find more appealing than what you wear now. If you find you cannot adapt to them, we will see if there isn't perhaps some form of trouser I can tolerate. I have no issue with the shirts by themselves."

His words cheered me.

"Come, there is food waiting for you."

I SPENT the remainder of the day wandering around the

manor and asking the beast questions about various rooms. Often he didn't answer or told me it wasn't my concern, but he made an effort to clear the mist when he spoke to me, and his growl faded as the day progressed.

The next morning, an unruffled day dress with no lace or other adornments waited hidden among several other options in the wardrobe. The drab brown color made me smile as I plucked it from its lace-bedecked companions.

When I stepped from the room, the beast made no comment. He followed me to the kitchen. Now, whenever I walked into the room, some form of food waited for me on the table. At the moment, eggs and thickly sliced bacon with mushrooms and cooked tomatoes waited on the tray.

"I never see you eat," I said as I sat at the chair. "When do you?"

"After you sleep."

I watched his eyes when he answered and saw them flick to the bacon.

"That seems a long time to go without food." Picking up a piece of bacon, I held it out to him. "Here," I offered holding it lightly.

He moved quickly, stretching from his mist and snapping it from my fingers in one bite that left me wide-eyed.

"I am not a tame pet," he said.

"Obviously," I said with a laugh. "A pet would have licked my fingers in thanks."

He made a choked noise, but I didn't look up from my food or offer him another bite.

After finishing every crumb on my plate, I stood with a content sigh.

"Is there a bag here that I could use? Like the one I used to own?" Before you shredded it, I thought sadly.

"I would like to walk the wall today and want something to carry the things I find."

"Look inside the servant's room."

I fetched the bag that I knew waited and held the door for him as we left. We spent the remainder of the day walking the wall, and he spent the majority of it without his mist.

CHAPTER THREE

I woke to a noise in my room and sat up abruptly. Weak moonlight and a dying fire cast shadows in the room, and I couldn't see more than vague shapes.

"Sir?" I called with my heart thundering.

Everything remained quiet, though I knew something had woken me. I held still for several long minutes until I heard the noise again. A rip and growl from the other side of the closed door.

I slipped from my bed and tiptoed toward the beast's door as noises continued from the other side. Carefully, I pulled the handle, and the door eased open. The fire in the room blazed; and within the light, I saw his massive form lying on the bed. He tossed about, his claws tearing the mattress as he struggled against a dream inspired foe.

"Sir?" I whispered again.

He shifted onto his back, and his struggles calmed

slightly, but I saw his hands still twitched. Approaching the bed, I tentatively reached toward him to smooth the hair on his arm. It stood up stiffly, an indicator of his mood.

When I looked up at his face, I saw the glint of his eyes as he watched me.

"A dream troubled you," I barely whispered, wondering if he would roar at me for the intrusion. Instead, he closed his eyes; so I continued to stroke his fur. When the fur on his arm gradually settled, I shifted to his head where it still stood up wildly.

He sighed loudly, looped an arm around me, and tugged me onto his bed. When I landed, a cloud of feathers erupted around us. I squeaked in surprise and dread. I didn't want to be in his bed, I'd only thought to ease his troubled mind.

"Stay until I sleep," he said, closing his eyes.

I relaxed slightly and shifted in the loose feathers to again stroke my fingers through the fur on his head. Not long after, I felt his body relax and his breathing deepen.

The beast confused me. During the day, I attributed his ire to his isolation since he only had me for company. Once I retired each night, I had given little thought to what he did. Yet, I should have. The state of his room on my first day should have told me just how troubled his nights might be.

A feather tickled my nose, and I softly blew it away.

What thoughts tormented him so much that he sought to destroy the comfort and extravagance around him?

Carefully, so I wouldn't wake him, I eased myself to the side of the bed and lightly touched my feet to the floor.

"She will never free me," he mumbled and rolled to his side.

"Who?" I whispered.

He didn't answer.

Looking at him, I decided he still slept. I withdrew from his room, leaving a trail of feathers. It was a long while before I slept.

SQUARING MY SHOULDERS, I dropped the beast's shirt to the floor and undid my braid.

After his comment the night before, I decided today would be the first day to try our new bargain. He'd let me wear proper clothes for two days and had let me see him without his mist. But it was last night, seeing him so disturbed by whatever he dreamt, that made up my mind. He had so many secrets, and no one to trust with them. I wasn't sure I wanted to be his confidant, but I didn't like being in the dark either. I hoped keeping my end of the bargain would open him up to a few questions I had. I wanted to know who wouldn't free him and from what he wanted to be freed.

As I stood combing my hair before the mirror, I began

to shiver. This would never work. I would shiver the whole day through and wake up sick in the morning, I thought to myself. Yet, I knew if I didn't try to uphold my end of our new bargain, I would find myself dressed in his choice of clothes once again. Taking a calming breath, I smoothed my hands over my hair. Unbraided, it fell to my waist and could serve to shield me a little if I chose. But I didn't use it that way.

With one last worried look at myself, I turned away from the mirror. Each step brought more doubt, and by the time I reached the door, my hand shook. I paused and took a fortifying breath before setting my hand on the handle. I pulled open the door.

In the hall, the beast looked up from his usual waiting place. Without the mist, I saw the shock on his face. Before I blinked, a storm cloud of mist erupted around him, swirling with an intensity that stirred the air around me.

"Do not move," he said.

I stood frozen with my hand still on the door handle. His reaction and the violence of the tempest that surrounded him robbed me of my thin courage. My limbs shook with cold and fear. Several long minutes passed with the mist growing no calmer.

"Beauty," he growled. "Lead and I will follow."

My voice failed me the first time I tried to speak. After clearing it, I managed a whisper.

"I would, but between fear and cold, I'm shaking too badly. May I try again tomorrow?"

"No." The single word sounded like a desperate plea. "I will meet you in the library. Join me when you are ready."

He departed quickly, leaving me stunned and clinging to the door. I wasn't sure what I'd expected, but the disturbing storm that had surrounded him hadn't been it. That he'd left me as soon as I'd mentioned my fear helped calm me.

I went back into my room and looked in my wardrobe for a wrap. It was empty of everything. Even the shirt I'd dropped on the floor had disappeared.

Wrapping my arms about myself, I shivered and awkwardly walked naked through the halls until I reached the library doors. They stood ajar and glowed with orange light. Inside, I heard the roar of a large fire. I peeked around the corner but saw no sign of the beast. Or of his mist. However, the curtains were drawn, making it hard to see very far into the room beyond the circle of fire light.

Darting inside, I stood before the fire and held out my hands to warm myself. It seemed the temperature inside had dropped severely since revealing myself.

A whisper of noise had me spinning. A great black cloud churned just inches from me.

"Eat," he said gruffly.

Only then did I notice the tray laden with every sweet imaginable. My stomach growled. The tray sat low on the table, and I didn't want to bend to reach it.

"Could I see you please?" I whispered.

When he had shown himself during those brief

periods over the last several days, he'd always appeared calm. The black air around him did not hint at calm. I needed to know what it meant.

"No," he said in a surprisingly gentle voice. "Eat. Do not fear me. You are safe."

I glanced at the tray. Everything on it tempted me, but it felt like a trap.

Taking a fortifying breath, I reached for a pastry glazed with sugar and stuffed with dates, ignoring the strawberries and grapes. I kept my eyes trained on the cloud the entire time, but nothing changed. It still swirled in the same position. I continued my wary study as I took my first bite. The sugar melted on my tongue, and the taste momentarily distracted me.

The mist moved away from me. I watched in surprise as it drifted toward the shelves and plucked the gilded book I'd wanted to read several days ago. The beast returned to the sofa and set the book on the cushions for me.

"Relax," he encouraged. "Read."

"I would prefer not," I said, not willing to turn my back on him.

He didn't become upset as I expected. Instead, he seemed to sense he caused my unease because he drifted from behind the sofa to the corner near the first curtained window.

"Please, sit," he said in a firmer tone.

Finishing the pastry, I licked my fingers and picked up the book. I sat as he bade and tried to read. I felt absurd sitting there naked while holding a book, and my mind drifted to my first glimpse of Father's classroom at the Whispering Sisters. Had he felt the same way sitting in a chair before a group of naked woman? Had they? I wondered if it became easier the more time they spent together.

The blaze kept the room warm enough that I didn't shiver, but it began to warm the tray of food too much. I looked up, noted the glistening moisture on the fruit, and reached for several. The tartness of the grapes and sweetness of the strawberries complemented each other. When I'd eaten those, I went back to reading. I'd only managed a few pages when my eyes drifted to the pastries. The heat from the fire had warmed them enough that they smelled freshly baked.

I glanced at the mist, but it remained the same. Since sitting, he hadn't made a sound.

I stretched forward and plucked another pastry from the tray. The tiny tart was no bigger than the palm of my hand. I nibbled at it slowly and read.

The gilded book contained a compilation of poetry from several authors. Most of the poems annoyed me as whining drivel from love struck fools, but a few provoked deep thought and required re-reading. After several chapters, I tossed the book aside and looked up at the cloud.

"I need a moment," I said softly, hoping he would understand.

He didn't move, so I stood and quickly left the library. I considered running to his room and getting a shirt but took a few calming breaths and made it back to my room to use the chamber pot, instead.

Away from the fire, I started shivering again. The cold didn't cause me to hurry, though, and my teeth chattered by the time I returned to the library.

I peeked around the door just to be certain the beast hadn't moved. The mist still swirled in the corner. I crept inside and stood before the fire, telling myself he was just sleeping and wouldn't notice me. Gradually, the shivers eased, and I sat on the sofa again. New food waited on the tray, cooled meat pulled from a bird and tender cooked vegetables.

I moved to the shelves to look for a different book. Since farming had held my interest for a while, I decided to read about animal husbandry. It amused me since I sat with a beast while reading it.

Losing track of time, I jumped slightly when the mist moved toward me, nudging the table. It momentarily blocked the view of the fire. The crash of a log and crackle of new flames explained why he'd moved. I hadn't thought of feeding the fire. With the table so close, I settled back into the sofa and nibbled while I read.

Hours later, I unfolded my legs, which I'd curled under me at some point and stretched with a huge yawn. The food tray was missing from the table, and the fire had burned down again. I recalled the beast moving several times to add to it, but he'd remained in the corner for the last hour.

Other than feeding the fire, he'd not moved or spoken to me the entire day. I still didn't feel comfortable without clothes, but I wasn't afraid anymore.

"Come," he said softly. He sounded strained. "I will walk with you to your room."

I led the way through the hallway, feeling his acute gaze, and tried not to run. When we reached the door, he followed me inside. Another tray waited with a steaming bowl of soup. I still felt full from the last tray even though the pink light of sunset radiated through the windows.

"Thank you for today, Benella. Perhaps tomorrow I will be able to repay you as you deserve."

I turned to see him withdraw and close the door.

The day hadn't been what I'd expected. Because of the lesson that Aryana and Ila had provided, I'd imagined myself running from him when his pent energies became too much. At the very least, I'd thought he would leave to find the wood nymph.

I opened the wardrobe and found the shirt I'd taken from him and slipped it on, glad to finally have cover.

THE BEAST DIDN'T WAIT in the hallway the next morning

when I exited my room, wearing another plain dress. I thought he might be tired of my company after the prior day. I would have grown bored watching me read, too.

Gliding through the silent hallways, I made my way to the kitchen ready to spend the day outside. Though I loved books, I loved being outdoors as well. When I'd peered out my window, the sun had been peeking through thin morning clouds, promising a mild day.

I entered a cold kitchen and glanced at the empty table in surprise. The beast paced before the door, his stormy mood apparent in his fur and bared teeth, which he chose not to hide from me. He muttered to himself quietly until I spoke.

"Sir?"

His head whipped toward me as if in surprise.

"I'm afraid yesterday was for nothing," he growled lowly.

I remained quiet, hoping he'd provide more information.

"In punishment for my failed attempt, she's blocked my ability to control the magic of this place since I could not control—"

He lashed out at the table in a violent rage. The wood split under the fury of his ravaging claws and a chunk flew toward me. In horror, I watched it tumble through the air. The wood piece struck my face just above the jawline, stinging as it gouged the skin before falling to the floor.

I gasped and pressed a hand to my face. The noise

DECEIT

penetrated his rage enough to pause his destruction. His ragged breathing filled the room as tears filled my eyes, mostly from anger not pain. My fingers felt warm and wet, and I pulled my hand away long enough to look at the blood.

Without saying a word, I walked toward him. His angry gaze met mine.

"You hurt me," I said flatly. I turned away and pulled open the outer door.

He made no move to follow me.

I strode through the long grass and made my way toward the gate as I wondered what level of stupidity had possessed me to think I might actually have had a positive influence on the beast. It was that tree's fault. Teach him, it had said. Some creatures couldn't be taught kindness, patience, or civility.

Tears trickled down my face, and I stumbled over a tree root. The cut burned now, but no more than I deserved for my conceit. I'd been so certain I'd be able to figure out the puzzle that surrounded the beast.

A roar sounded behind me, pulling me from my thoughts enough to see that all of the vines and roots of the trees around me quivered oddly. The roots in the path ahead of me flattened to the ground as if trying to help ease my passage. Good, I thought, hurrying. Behind me, the beast roared again. This time, it sounded more like a curse. Ahead, the gates beckoned, yawning wide. As I stepped through them, the beast roared my name.

In the distance, the rattle of an empty wagon bed reverberated through the trees. I hurried my steps, and several minutes later, my feet crunched on the gravel of the road toward the Water. Just rounding the bend from Konrall, a wagon driven by Henick slowed to avoid me.

Henick smiled and called softly to his team as he pulled back on the reins.

"Benella, what are you doing here? I thought you left with your family to settle in Water-On-The-Bridge."

His familiar friendly smile sent a wave of relief through me just as the beast again roared my name. Henick's mouth firmed as he looked at me closely.

"What happened?" he asked with true concern.

"I'm sorry to ask this of you, but can I ride with you to the Water? I had a run in with the beast." Better that he thought the beast knew my name from a trespass than from an extended stay.

"Of course." He set the brake and jumped from the seat to offer me a hand up.

"That cut looks deep," he said as I settled onto the seat. He pulled a clean square of cloth from his pocket, and reaching into the bed of the wagon, he used a water skin to soak it before handing it to me.

"Hold that to the cut."

I took the cloth and pressed it to my cheek as he climbed back into the seat and clucked the team into action again. The beast's roars faded as we moved away. I kept a wary eye on the vines, but they remained dormant.

"What are you doing so far from home?" he asked.

I sighed and told him as much of the truth as I could.

"Things weren't going well in Konrall so Father moved us to the Water, but the house there is too small. That's why he wanted Bryn and Blye to marry. But he wouldn't force them into a decision they weren't ready to make. So, we all moved into a one room home in town. We're struggling for food. I thought I could gather near the estate like I used to."

He nodded.

"Did Bryn marry?"

"No."

"I offered for her," he said.

I nodded and turned the cloth over, hoping for a cooler spot.

"Do you think she might reconsider?"

I sighed, thinking of her current troubles.

"She might. But you should know she put her hopes in a man who left her with no promises, only a babe."

"Children are a blessing," Henick said firmly.

I hoped Bryn would open her eyes if Henick offered for her again.

THE WAGON CLATTERED to a stop in front of the small cottage, and Henick quickly leapt down to help me from my seat. My face throbbed, so I waved him toward the front door as I walked around back to get cooler water from the well.

When I walked through the back door, I only caught Bryn's reply to Henick's question.

"I want no part of dirt farming and scraping to live from season to season. Now that I'm in the Water, I see how much I like town life. I plan to marry up, not down."

Henick nodded and turned without a word. Bryn closed the door and turned to see me standing there with my mouth open. Saying nothing, she marched to her room and closed the door. I ran to the front door and pulled it open, calling Henick's name just as he moved to climb into the seat.

He paused and waited for me to run to his side.

"You should keep that on the cut," he said lightly, taking the cloth from my hand and guiding it to my face.

"She's a fool," I whispered harshly, raising my hand to his cleanly shaven jaw. "Marrying you would be marrying up no matter what kind of life to which your wife is born." I leaned forward and kissed the cheek opposite of the one I held.

He smiled and took my hand to press it against the cloth on my jaw.

"Truthfully, her answer doesn't bother me. When I heard two of the Hovtel sisters were to be married, I'd hoped one would be you." He brushed a light kiss on my cheek. A blush ignited where his lips had touched and spread outward.

"Tell your father to contact me when it's your turn. I'd gladly be the first to offer for you."

When he turned to climb aboard, I found my voice.

"Why did you hope it was me?" I asked.

"We, my brothers and I, thought you might finally be ready to notice we existed," he said, grinning down at me.

What an odd thing to say, I thought.

"Of course I knew you existed."

His smile only widened.

I didn't know how to respond to that so, instead, I chose to change the subject.

"Did your father ever take you fishing after our visit?" If possible, he smiled wider.

"He did, and it was the best fishing. Ma dried what we couldn't eat that night and said it would make a fine soup come winter. He also received your note and sent a reply to your father. He teases Ma about wanting to catch a crow to train to carry messages." His smile faded a little. "It might seem like we live from season to season, but we don't scrape. The land Da's clearing is meant to build a house for the first son who marries."

"If you find someone before it's my turn, she'll be lucky to have you," I said quietly and backed up a step. He shook the reins and pulled away.

Instead of walking inside, I started down the road after him, walking in his dust. From the neighbor's roof, a crow cawed and clacked its beak at me.

"Quiet," I muttered, not wanting to acknowledge anything related to the beast just yet.

Covered with a cloak, Ila stood at the door when I rounded the back corner of the house.

"What happened?" she demanded and nudged the guard. He dutifully took a step toward me, but I held up a hand, motioning him to stay.

"I'm fine. I'm here because I need to speak with someone who still has an ounce of sanity."

She held out her hand and helped me up the remaining stairs. With the door closed, she shrugged out of the cloak then tugged me along. Instead of the basement, she turned down the hall to the right. Aryana waited inside a very clean room with a narrow bed.

"Well?" she said kindly.

"Well, what?"

"What happened to your face, dearest?"

"Oh. Carelessness. A piece of wood." I peeled the cloth away and showed her.

She tsked and motioned for me to sit on the bed. Using a clean cloth from a fresh bowl of water that waited on a nearby table, she washed the wound and pulled a sliver from the raw skin.

"I would say we should sew it, but I'm afraid there might be more splinters. If we sew them in, it would become infected. Best to let it heal on its own. It will likely leave a noticeable scar."

I nodded absently, thinking of Henick's comment. I'd

always noticed him and his brothers when they'd come to town. They were a lively bunch that never let the baker or the Coalres bother them. When they'd smiled and greeted me, I'd always smiled in return.

Frowning, I realized I'd never actually said anything in return. In fact, looking back, I realized I'd spoken very little, content with my own thoughts and observations. I compared myself to the beast. He kept his own counsel, and it frustrated me. Was that how Henick felt when I'd done the same to him? Very seldom had I spoken my mind. It wasn't until I met the beast that I started speaking what I thought. Even then, I still kept much to myself, like now.

I felt Aryana's curious gaze.

"I met a friend on the road who let me ride with him in his wagon. He made a curious comment. He said that he thought I might be ready to realize he existed." I met Aryana's gaze. "I've always known he was there. I've never really spoken to him, but I've always smiled in return whenever he's greeted me. Why would he think I ignored him?"

Ila laughed huskily and left the room. Aryana sat beside me and clasped my hand in her own. I interrupted whatever she was about to say with another question.

"Isn't it uncomfortable sitting bare bottomed?" I blushed when I realized what I'd said.

She smiled behind the veil.

"You sound as if you are speaking from experience."

"Curiosity will be my downfall," I said with forced playfulness.

"Yes, it is uncomfortable at first. Then I grew used to it, and no longer even notice. As for your friend, I think he meant you never noticed him in a way a woman notices a man."

"That's silly. I remember thinking him handsome the first time I saw him."

"And?" she prompted.

"And what?" I asked confused.

"Did he make your heart flutter or your insides melt?"

"No," I said slowly. "That sounds uncomfortable."

She laughed and patted my hand.

"It is, but in a pleasant way. Come, let's tell your father you're here. He will want to spend time with you."

FATHER and I walked together down the market street while I told him of Henick's opportune arrival and Bryn's second rejection of his offer. We talked of Blye's success at the dressmaker's and her talk of opening her own shop in the south. I knew that meant she hoarded her coin and felt pity for Father.

He made no comment about the cut on my face, but I knew he still worried.

As the streets filled with people, Father sighed and said he needed to return to work. I realized I had nowhere to go. I couldn't return to the Sisters as they were now accepting customers, and I didn't want to face Bryn after listening to her rude refusal.

Hugging Father good-bye, I started the walk back to the estate.

THE BEAST WAITED within the gates, making no attempt to hide himself.

"You returned," he said in relief when I stepped through the opening.

"Of course," I said stiffly. "I wouldn't want you dragging my father from his bed tonight when I didn't."

I marched past him in the direction of the manor, but he caught my skirt and spun me around.

"I apologize for hurting you," he said gruffly. "Let me heal it."

"No. I want to wear it as a reminder for you. I'm a person, not an object that will withstand your fury and repair itself. I am not part of this estate."

"I will not forget again."

"Pardon me if I don't believe you." I tugged my skirt from his clawed grasp and heard a rip. Not caring, I started on my way only to be snagged again.

"I'm not asking. Hold still so I can heal it."

Slowly turning, I glared at him and crossed my arms.

He approached me on all fours, a repentant look in his eyes.

"Bring back the wispy gowns. I will not stand before you without clothes again."

"Close your eyes," he ordered as if I hadn't spoken.

Exhaling angrily, I closed my eyes. The first swipe of his tongue over my jaw hurt, but the pain faded with each subsequent turn.

When he stopped, I opened my eyes and found the black mist surrounding us, too thick to see through. Something brushed over my collarbone. A knuckle perhaps? The gentle touch conflicted with the tumultuous mist.

"Rose, the enchantress, has cast a spell on me, and I'd hoped with your help to be free of it last night."

He turned away, and I quickly jogged to catch up, grabbing his tail. My curiosity outweighed my anger with him.

"How can I help free you?"

"I would rather talk inside," he said quietly.

The walk seemed to take longer. When he pushed inside the kitchen, I noticed that the table was still splintered but a loaf of bread was set on the block with a chair beside it.

"Sit and eat," he ordered.

"Will you tell me?" I asked, moving to the chair.

"She requires one night of pleasure," he growled, obviously agitated.

"And that is a problem?" After seeing him with the wood nymph, I wasn't sure how it posed a problem.

"Yes. If you recall, she's haggard and old," he replied dryly.

"I've met her?"

"Twice. I brought you to her cottage when you hit your head, and she brought the medicine when you were ill."

I vaguely recalled an older woman with missing teeth.

"How can I help?"

"If I could close my eyes and picture someone else, I thought I might have a chance. It worked until my first—"

I waited for him to continue but he did not.

"Your first what?"

"Never mind," he growled. "I should have known it wouldn't be so easy."

I ate quietly for several long minutes.

"You're trapped here and the only way to freedom is by giving this enchantress one night of pleasure," I said in summary, more for my benefit than his. "How long have you been here?"

"Over fifty years."

"You've been trying to pleasure her each night for over fifty years?" I asked in disbelief.

"Not every night. Several years ago she limited me to twice a week."

I felt a little gaggy on his behalf and understood why he would want to close his eyes and imagine someone else. Why me, though?

"It seems to me that if you've been trying the same thing for fifty years and getting the same disappointing results, you would try something different."

He sighed.

"That's why you're here. Now, I don't wish to talk about this anymore."

I immediately understood my role too well, but I doubted staring at me all day was enough to store up his energies to ensure an entire night of the old woman's attentions. But thanks to the sisters, I had a few more ideas.

"One more question," I said. He nodded reluctantly. "Will you allow me to help you?"

"I already have."

The humor in his tone was unmistakable, and I knew he meant walking around naked the day before.

CHAPTER FOUR

"No. I can truly help you," I said.

The first thing I needed to do was calm him. His rages were dangerous to me, and undoubtedly disadvantageous to his goal to free himself. However, I felt the sisters' techniques for muscle relief, given Gen's response, might lead to another chase through the woods. Perhaps a bath, then?

I glanced at the beast and found him watching me closely. His fur stuck up in odd places and some burrs clung to his tail. No doubt, he would need convincing to get into a tub.

Standing, I marched toward him and leaned in to sniff.

"You need a bath," I said. "Come. I think you'll fit in one of the washtubs in the laundry."

"I'm not bathing."

"I'll help," I said.

The world spun, and I found myself clinging to his back. As soon as he lurched forward, I fisted my hands in his fur and wrapped my legs around his waist. He raced around a few corners and suddenly we stood in the laundry.

Sliding off his back, I grinned at the beast.

"That was fun. I'd expected there to be a fire and hot water when we arrived, though."

"I believe I mentioned she blocked my ability to use the magic."

"No matter," I said as I bent to start the fire.

Behind me, I heard him lifting the large pots to fill with water. We worked together for a long while before we had one of the tubs half filled with steaming water.

"In you go," I said.

He turned away from me and stepped into the water with a hiss. I quickly poured in another bucket of cooler water so he could sit. He sighed when he submerged up to his chest, his knees spread wide.

Using a dipper, I wet all of his fur and began lathering him. Once his fur was plastered against his skin, I could easily feel the hard ridges of his muscles. They distracted me from my purpose, and I found my hands idly wandering over their expanse. Recalling Ila's instruction, I began to wash him, rubbing the tension from the muscles in his shoulders and torso.

After I rinsed his back, I moved to the side of the tub and encouraged him to lift first one leg then the other out of the water. He watched me closely as I worked. I likewise paid close attention to him, ready to bolt if he showed any sign of pent energies.

Under the guise of scrubbing, I rubbed his calf muscles and as much of each thigh as I could reach under the water. Several times, I bumped into something under the murky depths, but didn't know if it was his penis or ball sack. Either way, the flesh did not feel firm, so I continued my efforts to ease his tension.

I didn't speak as I worked, preferring to adopt the sisters' silence. It gave me an opportunity to contemplate how to broach the subject of his failed attempts with Rose and what he might try differently. I hoped, after the bath, he'd be more open to suggestions.

When I moved to his head, he groaned and laid it back against the edge of the tub. He kept his eyes closed and his arms relaxed on the edge of the tub as I worked, and I felt certain I'd succeeded in calming him.

After rinsing him a second time, he rose from the tub and shook himself, sending water spraying everywhere. I gasped in surprise and felt doubly shocked when he laughed at me. A real laugh.

"Let's finish drying in the library," I suggested, wondering how long he'd stay relaxed and, hopefully, receptive to conversation.

He followed me closely and used the mist to cloak himself. In the library, I waited until he once again settled in the corner before speaking.

"I have a proposal. I know when aroused, you have certain pent energies..."

He made a choking noise.

"...that need to be released or you become tense and angry. However, have you considered that releasing these pent energies might be counterproductive toward your goal of a full night with the enchantress?"

"It crossed my mind as I sat in this very corner yesterday," he said sardonically.

"I'm speaking of a larger sacrifice," I said, excited that he understood and seemed willing to discuss the topic. "You've been doing the same thing for fifty years. What if you did not visit the enchantress for a week or two while letting your energies build? It might give you an advantage."

"A week," he scoffed.

"I'll help you. You just need to stay focused on the goal —your freedom."

He remained quiet in the corner for so long I began to pace. Perhaps, I'd assumed too much by speaking openly of his physical needs. It seemed that no one actually spoke of that in polite conversation, discounting the sisters of course.

"Perhaps, you're right," he said slowly. "This could work."

I stopped pacing and smiled at him.

"And, I suppose you want something in return for your help?" he said mulishly.

I fought not to roll my eyes.

"Not everything needs to be a trade or part of some deal. I'm helping to be helpful. That's all." And, maybe, by being so, I would win my own freedom.

He grunted, but said nothing more.

Several days later, I struggled to maintain my temper as I faced the beast over breakfast. He paced back and forth in front of the door, his familiar mist cloaking him.

The day before he'd tried excusing himself often. However, each time I had quickly followed him, certain that he would try to find the wood nymph or some other substitute.

Now, he was surly and seemed to no longer care if I stayed at the estate or chose to flee. He had ordered me to take my day to visit my family.

"You can't order me to do that," I said. "I choose the day I visit."

For a moment, he paused his pacing to face me. An angry spark lit his eyes. When he resumed his pace, I set my fork down and quickly rose from my chair, ready to run if there seemed a need.

"You bore me, and I want time alone," he said with impatience and anger.

"Sir," I said, trying for a calm, soft voice. "It has only been a few days. Think of your freedom."

"I'm tired of thinking of it," he roared at me with such passion that his breath fluttered my hair.

"Let's go for a walk outside," I said, trying a different approach.

He spun toward me and took a step with each word he spoke.

"I do not want to walk outside. I want to fuck." He stood nose to nose with me, his breath fanning my face.

"Precisely why we need to calm you," I said, sensing my dangerous position.

He studied me for a long moment, then his tongue darted out to lap at my neck. I squeaked in surprise. He growled in response and stood on two legs, pulling me close. I only reached the bottom of his sternum when he stood, and his fur pressed into my face. I felt the length of his penis between my breasts.

He arched into me. I would have fallen backward if not for his arms holding me steady.

"Stop," I ordered him, trying to pull away. My movement only seemed to excite his thrusting. "You're hurting me." His root was bruising my ribs, and I felt a stab of pity for the wood nymph who had endured him. He was too large.

When he didn't listen, I stomped on first one paw, then the other. He roared but pulled away from me, dropping to all fours.

"There will be no fornicating," I yelled at him.

We glared at each other for a moment, then his temper

erupted. He lashed out and flipped the table over, sending the dishes flying. This time, I covered my face to prevent injury. When he finished his fit and stood there panting, I retreated.

"I think I will visit my family," I said as I darted past him and out the door.

"Men aren't the only ones to suffer pent energies," he yelled at me as I ran.

I didn't know what he meant by that, but didn't slow to ponder it.

By the time I reached the gate, which swung open for me, I was out of breath and had a stitch in my side. The beast roared in the distance again. He still hadn't regained control of the estate, and it seemed to frustrate him as much as his pent energies.

I sprinted through the trees until I came to the gravel road and slowed to a hitched walk. Perhaps we were going about this wrong. He didn't respond well to self-denial. Perhaps I should have started with something smaller, like using the word "no" more often.

As I walked, I became aware of the sound of a wagon approaching from behind and turned to see Henick again.

I waved as he pulled up beside me.

"Going to the Water?" I asked.

Henick greeted me with a smile.

"I didn't think I'd see you again so soon." He jumped from the seat. "Your face is healed," he said in surprise and reached out to run a finger along my jaw.

"Yes, I'm very fortunate it didn't scar."

His touch left a slight tingle, and I blushed. Yet, the beast's parting comment rang in my ears. Why didn't I suffer from pent energies? Aryana had also hinted that I should feel my heart flutter or some such nonsense. Was I defective?

"Henick, why did you think I didn't notice you?"

He smiled again and lowered his hand, holding it out to me instead. I wrapped my sweat-dampened fingers around his warm, dry ones as I accepted his assistance and climbed up to the seat.

"Because you never lingered," he said easily, moving around the team to get to his side of the bench. "You never stopped to watch us like we stopped to watch you."

"Watch me?" I echoed, thinking of Tennen's words the night he'd waited for me in the dark. Was this what he'd meant? He'd been angry because I'd never noticed him?

Henick laughed and shook his head at me.

"Everyone stops to watch you when you walk through the village, Benella."

That made me feel a bit uncomfortable.

"Is there something wrong with me?" He looked at me with worry. "Not that everyone watches me," I clarified quickly, "but that I don't watch back."

He smiled again, a small, soft smile.

"I don't think so. I think you're waiting for the right moment."

I frowned, and he laughed.

"You think before you feel," he said.

As I considered his words, I knew he was right.

We rode the rest of the distance in silence, and I asked him to drop me off by the mill so I could walk the rest of the way. When he slowed the team, I turned to kiss his cheek again. However, he turned at the same time and our lips met. A tingle of shock ran through me, and I pulled back in surprise.

Henick chuckled at my expression.

"Have you ever been kissed?" he asked.

"I have now," I mumbled.

"I'm honored to be the first," he said. He made no move to claim another one. I felt sure if it were the beast beside me instead of Henick, I would be fighting for my freedom.

Beside us, a crow cawed from a post bordering the mill. I stared at it as I licked my lips.

"Thank you, Henick," I said quietly, jumping to the ground before he could move to help me.

"Perhaps I'll see you on the road again," he said in farewell and encouraged the team forward.

I watched him disappear down the lane and, lost in thought, started toward the market district. A familiar laugh drew me from my reverie as I passed a baker's stall.

Bryn stood with the baker's son in quiet discussion, leaning toward him and touching his arm lightly. He looked similar to Tennen. The young man's eyes repeatedly dipped to Bryn's cleavage, and his blush deepened each time.

Bryn spied me and said a quick, shy farewell to the man before walking my way. I waited for her, glad she wore a smile for a change. She looked much prettier for it.

"He's the one," she whispered, hooking her arm through mine. We walked toward home.

"What one?" I asked.

"The one who will offer for me. Edmund Rouflyn. His father runs the most successful bakery in the Water. It's just the two of them."

"I'm so happy for you, Bryn." I hugged her side. "Is he excited for the baby?"

She dug her fingers into my arm.

"Quiet," she hissed.

I frowned at her, not understanding her change in mood at first. Then, it dawned on me.

"You haven't told him?"

"He looks a lot like Tennen. He will never know it's not his because we've already been together," she whispered to me as she smiled and nodded to someone else in the market. "And he's much better than Tennen, too." She glanced at me from the corner of her eye. "You wouldn't know anything about that yet, would you," she said with a sigh.

Not knowing how to respond to that, I asked about Blye.

"She's doing well enough. Her dresses are selling, but slowly. Father's still trying to marry her off. She's getting offers but isn't in a position where she needs to settle like me."

Bryn was in a chatty mood and didn't give me any opportunity to excuse myself until it was well past ten. I knew the sisters were already taking clients, so I spent a long, boring day with my sister, who repeatedly begged me to bring something of value to trade the next time I visited.

When she began to prepare dinner, she politely told me there wasn't enough for four. I excused myself to meet Father on his way home.

I told him of Bryn's hope of the baker's son, and he nodded, sharing my concerns. He was disappointed he'd missed the opportunity to visit with me but was glad I'd spent time with Bryn. I left him with a kiss on his cheek and began the walk back to the estate.

WHEN I RETURNED, the kitchen was quiet and still destroyed. I skirted the wreckage and cautiously wandered the halls, speculating on the mood in which I would find the beast. Near the study, I heard an odd clicking noise. I stilled in the hallway, listening intently. It sounded like a tap of something against the glass.

Peering around the door, I watched in amazement as the beast threw open a window to let the crow in. The crow sat on the sill and cawed several times, clacking his beak in between caws. The beast watched him in silence, his fur slowly standing on end.

Beyond the crow, the sight of the wood nymph distracted me from the pair. Solid, she remained bent at the waist, her hair-like branches trailing the ground. As I watched, the spring green leaves from her hair fluttered to the earth in slow solidarity. The bark of her torso looked thin and curled in some places as if peeling away. The trunk of one leg glistened wetly. She looked broken.

The crow took flight, startling a noise from me as the beast rounded on me.

"You kissed him?" he roared.

The wood nymph trembled outside.

"You are mine," he growled, stalking toward me.

I stepped forward, meeting him without fear.

"Kiss me as you did him."

"No," I shouted, angry. He needed to be told no regardless of our agreement. "I'll end up broken or worse. Look at her!" I gestured at the wood nymph through the window. "If she were human, she would be ripped and bleeding. You are a beast. You don't stop and think how your actions might affect others. You have no regard for anyone but yourself and your own satisfaction."

He was no longer listening to me but stood before the window, staring at the nymph.

"Human," he said, before spinning from the window and racing from the room on all fours.

I glanced out the window in confusion. More leaves fell

from the nymph's hair, and I wondered how many times he'd taken her.

The beast turned the corner at a run. When he reached her solidified form, he began speaking in earnest whispers. I couldn't hear the words, but the nymph came to life and collapsed to the ground. The beast scooped her into his arms and ran out of sight.

I shook my head. He needed to think with something other than his root.

I didn't see him again for three days. All the while, a storm lashed at the manor.

WHEN THE STORM FINALLY CLEARED, I grabbed the bag from the servant's quarters, dressed in my trousers and shirt, and strode out into the tranquil, dripping wet world. The sun made a valiant effort to break through the thick clouds above, but I knew it wouldn't succeed. It was magic that had made the storm, and only magic would clear it.

I left through the front gate with no intention of going very far. It wasn't my day to visit my family. I wanted to walk the wall as I used to and see if there was anything I could gather for Bryn. Since the beast wasn't there to ask, I decided to try it without his permission.

Turning west, so I would visit the enchanted patch of ground last, I started my long walk. A caw from above didn't surprise me, and I looked up to see the crow hop from branch to branch to keep up with me.

"I thought we were friends. How could you tell him I kissed Henick when you saw exactly what happened? It was an accident, and nothing came of it." I scowled at the bird as it cawed again. "I suppose you're going to fly off now and tell him I left. This, too, is innocent. Just a walk around the wall out of boredom. But go ahead, tattle." I waved it away, but it stuck to me doggedly. So, I ignored it.

The wall offered me a bunch of primrose on the north side and cabbage at the patch of raw earth. Happy with my findings, I rounded the wall toward the gate. The crow cawed loudly in warning, and I saw the beast standing just within the gates.

"Where have you been?" he demanded.

"Ask Mr. Crow," I said, slipping through the gates to walk past him.

The crow cawed once and flew away. The beast followed me back to the manor and continued to follow me for the rest of the day. I didn't speak again.

WHEN I WOKE in the morning, the gossamer dresses were back. I glared at them then went to yank open my door. The beast waited without his mist. I stood before him, dressed in his shirt.

"No." I said the single word with finality.

"Yes," he returned calmly. "Go put on one of the dresses. I will try again."

"I refuse," I said, crossing my arms. "The problem with your plan is that you're too used to getting your way. You need to learn how to contain yourself when someone refuses you. Until you can, I will dress as I please, not as you please."

He growled at me, an angry light filling his eyes. Then he huffed out a breath and rubbed a paw over his face.

"You are correct. I need to learn control," he said as a haunted look came to his eyes. "Dress as you please."

He turned to stalk away, but I stopped him.

"Were you so horrible as a man?" I asked.

"You know?" he asked, sounding strained.

"I guessed, but now I know."

He turned and walked away.

When I opened the wardrobe, it offered something of every style. The sheer gowns were there as were the plain ones that would cover me. But I also spotted trousers and shirts. I smiled and dressed as I pleased, knowing the beast's control of the magic had returned.

I FOUND HIM MUCH LATER, pacing outdoors near the place the wood nymphs had favored. He didn't seem to hear my approach, and I paused to study him.

Weeks ago, I would have considered his back and forth

movement a prowl. Now, I saw his frustration in the bend of his ears, his guilt in the droop of his tail, and his hopelessness in the weary set of his great shoulders. How could I not feel pity for such a creature?

"How is she?" I asked.

He stopped his pacing and turned toward me.

"Healing." Regret laced that single word.

"If I continue to help you, I need your word that Rose alone will be the recipient of your attentions."

His gaze dropped to the ground beside him. Tiny leaves dotted the area. Her hair.

"You have my word."

The words barely reached my ears, but it was enough. I cleared my throat and set my resolve. I would help him.

"Can I still do as I please?" I asked.

He snorted in response.

"Given your refusal to listen to any command I make, I would say yes."

"Perfect. I'll return before dinner," I spun away with the hope that he'd wonder what I intended.

I didn't walk very far, my bag gently tapping against my hip, when I heard him follow. There were a few things we'd misunderstood when trying abstinence to help his chances with the enchantress. His willpower and his boredom. He had too much of one and not enough of the other.

Now, I planned to coax him from his shadows of observance into the light of participation. It most likely wouldn't work, and he would roar and growl and leave in a storm, but the more we tried, the more I learned about him. I felt certain I'd eventually learn enough to truly help him.

Marching north, I ambled through fallow fields and quiet forests until I came to the wall. Unlacing my boots, I tossed them to the ground and began to climb one of the trees that stretched over the stacked stones.

"You're going to fall. Get down," he called to me as I climbed out of his reach.

Laughing, I kept climbing up and up until I reached the thinner branches of the canopy. I looked to the south, and far in the distance, I saw a bit of roofline. To the northwest, the moving waters of the river twinkled in the sunlight. I looked down at the beast.

"Are you able to leave these walls?"

"Yes," he said suspiciously, "Why?"

I crossed my legs around the branch and started scooting forward toward the empty space that separated me from my destination. I loosened my legs and dangled from the branch to squat on top of the wall.

"Then come on."

He looked up at me with concern.

I slipped over the wall and out of his sight. Slowly, I worked my way down the wall, one foot and handhold at a time. The beast sailed over the wall, his back feet clipping it with a thunk, before I reached the ground.

"Impressive," I said, looking up at the top of the wall

that towered above my head. "You can clear it in one jump?"

"Yes, when necessary," he said, sniffing the air. "Why are we outside the estate? It isn't safe."

I scoffed at his concern. He was an enchanted beast. What had he to fear? I briefly thought of the stories of hunters and pillagers who'd tried to come for him in the past then quickly started walking away from the wall.

"You'll see why. It's a bit further. Come on."

We walked for another hour before the sound of the river reached my ears. My bare feet were starting to hurt, and I regretted not bringing the boots in the bag. But, I'd worried they would cause me to lose my balance on the tree.

Finding a quiet inlet, I stripped two branches for poles, attached the string and hooks I'd discovered in the bag, and handed one to the beast. I sat on a rock at the river's edge and dangled my feet into the cool water. The beast stood beside me, holding the pole uncertainly for a moment, then he joined me.

We sat in companionable silence for several hours while the fish ate our worms and laughed at our efforts. With the sun overhead, I pulled my hook from the water and opened my bag, hungry for the bread and cheese I'd taken from the kitchen.

Reaching to offer the beast half of the food, I watched him study the water. His eyes darted over the surface, following the shadows of the fish underneath.

"This is pointless," he growled.

I smiled at his frustration. "It's how most people eat every day," I said, handing him the food. "Haven't you ever had to work for your food?"

He scowled at me, but he accepted what I offered.

"There's something about it," I said. "A savory flavor to the food I gather with my own hands."

I watched him bite into the bread, and I considered it our first meal together. After eating, he grew restless, and I suggested we head back for a game in the library. He padded beside me, not commenting when I winced after stepping on something sharp. With sore feet, the climb back over the wall looked daunting.

"You control the vines, correct?" I said, staring at the high stone barrier.

"Yes," he said, watching me.

I turned to him with a mischievous smile.

"Toss me over the wall like you did the first time we met. Let the vines catch me."

He shook his head but gripped my waist with both hands a moment before flinging me up and over the wall. I laughed the whole way and landed on a loosely woven vine net. He sailed over the wall in one smooth vault.

"We should make a game of that," I said, still laughing as I jumped lightly to the ground and sat to tug on my boots. "It would be fun in water, too, when it's warmer. The splashes I could make." My mind wandered to the calculations of angles and heights needed until I caught his stare.

"You are not like other women," he said slowly, as if just realizing it.

Shaking my head at him, I stood and dusted off the seat of my trousers.

"A good thing for you, I am not."

DURING THE NEXT SEVERAL DAYS, I discovered something. The beast knew many games of chance, but very few intellectual ones. We studied a book of games and learned a few together. We made an odd pair sitting quietly in the library for hours, he on his haunches on the floor and me perched in a chair.

His mind was a beautiful thing to behold. He challenged me in a way that made me smile and laugh. But after mastering a game, he quickly grew bored with it whether he won or lost. The games of chance never lost his interest, though.

I studied him as he contemplated the wood board before us. He seemed relaxed and content, and I wondered if he knew how many days he'd gone without seeing the enchantress. Would it be enough?

Loathe to bring it to his attention, I continued to try to keep him constantly busy. As the days had stretched, I had watched for signs of growing agitation. As I'd guessed, boredom was his worst enemy.

Though four days had passed since I'd returned from my last visit to the Water, the games still served us well. However, I knew he would not tolerate another day of them.

"Have you ever wagered on a game?" I asked softly, not wanting to disturb his concentration.

"Certainly," he said absently.

"Would you care to wager on the outcome of this game?"

His gaze rose from the board to study me. "What kind of wager?"

"The food is delicious, but I think, if I should win, I want you to prepare my breakfast. By hand. Yourself."

"And if I win?"

I quirked a grin.

"Then I will prepare your food for you in the morning."

He chuckled and nodded, but I could sense his disinterest in the bet. I smothered my smile. It wasn't about winning or losing, but distracting him for another day.

I woke early and loudly.

"I'm so hungry," I called as I sat up in bed.

From the adjoining room, I heard a thump and knew I'd woken him. Light was just starting to filter into my room. We'd stayed up late to finish the game, which I'd won.

Of one thing I was absolutely certain. The beast couldn't cook.

Smiling, I dressed in a plain gown—I'd been favoring the trousers and shirt since our hike to the river—and washed my mouth and face before walking out into the empty hallway.

Following the sounds of clanking and muffled curses, I found him in the kitchen. The fire roared, warming the room a bit much, so I opened the door to the outside before moving out of the way.

From the chair near the table, I watched him bumble around. He dropped eggs on the floor and seared one side of the bacon black. He lost a potato in the fire and singed his fur trying to get it back out.

When he set a plate before me, we both blinked at the mess that smeared its surface.

"It looks delicious," I said after a moment.

"I don't know how to cook," he admitted with a defeated note.

Finally, honesty from him. I grinned.

"Neither do I. Well, maybe a tad more than you, but not much. I think I saw a book in the chef's room that could help us."

We spent the whole day in the kitchen, making some wonderful mistakes. He even laughed once when he sampled my attempt at a pastry. That laugh marked the first time I'd ever seen him without a hint of his usual anger and frustration. A rush of pride filled me at my accomplishment. There was something more to the beast, after all.

As I grew tired and yawned, he determinedly kept reading and cooking until he caught me with my head on the table.

"Perhaps, that's enough for today," he said, walking toward me.

I stood with agreement and looked at the disaster we'd made of the kitchen.

"Do we need to clean this?"

"No."

Relieved, I kissed him affectionately on the cheek and turned to leave the kitchen.

He stared after me as I walked away, but he made no move to follow. The dull greys and purples of dusk painted the sky. Perhaps he would see the enchantress tonight.

CHAPTER FIVE

When I met him in the hallway the next morning, he wore pants and stood upright. I made no comment, but greeted him with a smile and my usual question about our plans for the day. His only remark was that we should eat first.

As he led me to the kitchen, I marveled at his full height. I'd seen it before but never for so long. He typically dropped back to all fours after several steps. He suddenly seemed more man than beast.

He motioned me toward the table where I saw two plates set. Scrambled eggs and bacon rested on each. A simple meal...but not. He'd cooked.

The eggs were a little moist, and the blackened edges of the bacon strips contrasted with the limp middle. Instead of seeing the improvements still needed, I saw the progress he'd made.

"This looks marvelous," I said, and I meant it.

He held the chair for me as I sat, which surprised me, and joined me at the table. The chair groaned under his weight, but it held.

The eggs were cold and a bit on the salty side, but I ate them all. I couldn't have done better. Though I preferred crisp bacon, I managed to eat most of that as well. Leaning back, I thanked him for the effort.

"I wanted to thank you," he said. "For your help. Five days..." He shook his head and sighed. "It didn't work," he admitted.

I reached across the table and touched his hand.

"I'm so sorry. We'll keep trying." I hesitated a moment, then asked a hard question.

"Can you tell me what went wrong? It would help to know what we might need to change."

He laughed self-deprecatingly.

"Your amusements and distractions worked too well. I went to her door; but when she opened it expectantly, I could only apologize and bid her good night."

"Nothing?" I asked, stunned.

"Nothing that could inspire me to cross her threshold."

I chewed my lip for a while. How to keep his arousal without the anger and tension? The question was beyond my expertise. I needed to talk to the sisters but didn't think it wise to leave him dejected again. It took too long to walk there and back. A ride from Henick would be nice, but I couldn't count on that coincidence.

"Do you own a horse?" I asked with idle hope.

"There is a horse, yes," he said, obviously curious why I'd asked.

"I would like to visit the Water before we try again, but I don't want to leave you alone so long, and I doubt I would find a wagon on the road again."

He scowled at the reminder of Henick and agreed that a horse would help me journey faster. He left the table to stalk outside, and I dashed to the servant's quarters to fetch my bag. The primrose I'd picked lay pressed between waxed pages of a small book I'd found. I hadn't forgotten Bryn's request and hoped to stop in Konrall at the candle maker before journeying to the Water.

Slinging the bag across my body, I stepped outside. The beast stood before a quivering horse, speaking to it in a soft growl.

When he saw me, he stepped away and offered me a hand. We never afforded our own mounts, but I recalled riding a horse in my youth and peered at this one curiously.

"No reins?" I questioned the beast while clasping his hand.

"Speak to him, and he will do as you say," the beast assured me.

I placed my right foot in the beast's free hand and sprung upward, swinging my left leg forward over the horse's neck and almost kicking the beast in the head.

"I apologize," I said quickly to both of them as I

wrapped my fingers around the mane to keep myself upright.

Beside me, the beast rested a hand on my leg, his fingers heavy and twitching.

"Where are your underclothes?" he asked in a nearly unintelligible growl.

"I haven't the faintest idea. You haven't put them back in the wardrobe since I arrived. If you're willing to provide them again, I'm eager to wear them. I do feel a bit awkward without them at times."

The horse nickered and dipped its head. The beast reacted immediately, cuffing the creature upside its long head. It sidestepped from the blow.

"Sir," I cried. "What are you doing? Perhaps, I shouldn't go."

"I apologize. It would be best if you both leave for a short while." The beast spoke with slow effort.

He grabbed the horse's face in his large paw and brought its nose to his own.

"Protect her with your life."

The beast held the horse's gaze until it bobbed its head.

"Does he have a name?" I asked cautiously, still unsure of the beast's mood.

The beast released the horse and stared at it for a moment.

"If he does, I long ago forgot it."

"No matter," I assured him, patting the horse's neck to

get its attention. "For this journey, I shall call you Swiftly. Please take me to the gate, Swiftly."

The horse pivoted and started down the path. Turning, I looked back at the beast.

"I will return shortly. If you feel angry, perhaps you would consider making pastries," I said with a smile. We had yet to master those.

The beast nodded and continued to watch us as I turned forward again. Despite my promise to return shortly, I wondered if he continued to have concern that I might not return. I hoped that he had gained a measure of trust in me by now. Still, I didn't want to take any longer than necessary.

Swiftly's current pace, however, would be a problem. He walked softly and slowly, as if not wanting to jostle me. An additional brief stop in Konrall wouldn't be wise if he couldn't move faster.

"Am I too heavy?" I asked, unsure if an enchanted horse could bear as much of a burden as a normal horse.

Swiftly shook his head.

"Perhaps we could try a trot, then?" I suggested.

He immediately picked up the pace, and I had to clench my thighs around him to keep upright. He skittered nervously at the touch but kept moving.

Once we reached the gate, I asked him to head south instead of west. He balked a bit but eventually did.

Seeing Konrall again brought forth a tiny bit of homesickness. The lewd attentions of the baker and the bullying focus of Tennen and Splane had faded from my mind, and I recalled the better times when I went to school with Father, and Bryn and Blye talked to me about boys.

"See the candle maker's sign?" I asked softly. One of Swiftly's ears twitched back, and I knew he heard me. "That's where I need to stop. Then we ride to Water-On-The-Bridge."

Swiftly stopped before the candle maker's home and knelt so I could dismount with ease. And probably so I wouldn't expose myself. I patted his neck.

"A true gentleman," I whispered.

He dipped his head, and I smiled.

"Do you need water?"

He shook his head, so I left him to go inside.

"Benella! Good to see you. Come in, sit," the candle maker said, greeting me as if I were an old friend. He rocked to a stand, his wispy hair fluttering with his efforts.

"Good morning," I returned politely. "I've brought you more primrose." Withdrawing the small book from my bag, I carefully removed the drying flowers and set them on his table.

"Perfect," he breathed, lifting one delicate flat bloom to his nose. "You've preserved their scent."

He shuffled to his shelves and searched until he produced a blunt silver and a few copper, which he brought to me.

"This is all I have for now. The merchant promised a

higher sale for more of them, so I'll pay you more after he sells them."

"It's not necessary," I said. If he gave all his coin to me, how would he live until the merchant returned?

"Nonsense," he said, taking my hand and curling my fingers around the coins.

He gave me a narrow stare until I nodded. I dared not say more.

I thanked him, and we spent a few moments trading idle pleasantries. He asked after Father and any news from the Water. Awkwardly, I mentioned a few events I recalled Father mentioning during my last visit, but I left the details vague and hoped the candle maker wouldn't notice.

Though the nearby villages knew of the estate and avoided it, I wanted no one to know of my stay there. Too many coveted the riches they imagined the estate held, and greed motivated the kindest person to acts they might normally not commit.

Saying a hasty farewell and promising to return should I find more primroses, I escaped his innocent questioning.

Outside, Swiftly nickered when he saw me and knelt again to let me mount. Amused, I carefully swung my leg over his back and held on to his mane as he stood again.

"Benella," a familiar voice called from nearby.

I tensed on Swiftly, and the horse's left ear pivoted back in my direction as he swung his head toward the speaker. His flank quivered under me, and I ran a hand on his neck to soothe him as I watched the baker step off his porch to approach us. Despite the baker's extra girth, he carried himself with strength and speed.

"Good morning," I said with forced politeness.

"It's so good to see you, Benella," he said reaching out to pat my leg.

Swiftly sidestepped me out of reach and snorted at the baker. The baker dropped his hand, but not his eyes, which swept over me.

"You look well. You've gained some needed weight." He smiled slyly as his gaze lingered on my breasts. Swiftly's haunches quivered in earnest, and he backed up a step. The baker returned his gaze to mine and some of his humor faded.

"It's good to know you're being cared for," he said. His tone indicated otherwise, and I remained silent.

"I hope to visit the Water in two days and wanted to discuss some business with your father. Can you tell him to expect me for dinner?"

My stomach turned at the thought of what they might discuss. Thankfully, I wouldn't be there.

"Of course. Good day."

Swiftly took the cue and turned away from the baker.

"I will see you soon," the baker called in farewell.

"Not likely," I said as Swiftly picked up the pace, trotting north.

When we passed the smith's, Tennen stepped from the shadow of his father's forge with a rock in his hand.

"Run, Swiftly," I whispered urgently, leaning over the creature's back.

He didn't hesitate, but jumped into a full gallop. Clinging to his mane, I twisted to see Tennen pull back his arm. However, the sudden thunder of Swiftly's hooves had brought the butcher to his door; and he yelled for Tennen to stop. Caught, Tennen dropped the rock with a scowl.

Swiftly raced north and only slowed when we again neared the estate. I patted his neck and thanked him for his effort and protection. He bobbed his head in response, and we walked the rest of the way to the Water. Having a horse cut the travel time in half.

Worried that Swiftly would tell the beast of my activities, I brought him to the livery and gave a boy a copper to watch him for the short time I planned to stay. Swiftly nickered at me as if calling me back, but he remained with the boy, and I walked to the Whispering Sisters unobserved.

Ila met me at the door as usual.

"Benella, you look well."

"As do you," I said, accepting her hug while trying not to act self-conscious about where I placed my hands on her bare back.

"You have purpose in your eyes," she said when she pulled away. "What brings you here?"

"I seek advice," I said. "The kind only you and Aryana are likely to give."

She nodded sagely and led me to the bathing

chambers. Aryana stood when I entered, but I waved her back to the water.

"Please sit. I would enjoy a bath," I said, thinking of the baker's stare and the ride to get there, "but I promised my employer my jaunt would be brief."

Aryana eased back into the water while Ila and I relaxed on a cushion. My skirts seemed so out of place, but they didn't appear to mind.

"What do you need of us?" Aryana asked.

"I need to know how to attract and hold a man's attention in a way to inspire arousal without the tension or aggression."

Aryana studied me quietly, her mouth turned down ever so slightly.

"Are you sure?" she whispered with concern.

"I'm sure of nothing," I replied with a slight smile. "But I'd like your advice regardless."

She considered me for another moment before speaking.

"Arousal is easy. A bit of flirting and an accidental glimpse of your breast or elsewhere would achieve that state. To prolong that state without tension is a bit difficult. You need to find a way to keep it light. Entertaining. A game, in which you both willingly play."

A game. He did well with games. Perhaps something with betting. I chewed my lip as I thought about the options. The biggest concern was keeping his arousal in check so the enchantress was the target and not myself.

The image of the wood nymph rose to mind. This new game would be dangerous.

"Thank you," I said and stood. "I will see you again soon, I'm sure." I was embarking into unexplored territory, after all, and would undoubtedly have more questions.

"A moment," Aryana whispered, stopping me. "Benella, have you ever flirted?"

I couldn't see her eyes clearly, but I saw the amusement in her smile.

"No," I admitted. "But I've watched others. I'm sure I can manage a few unintelligent, insipid remarks."

Ila burst out in a deep laugh while Aryana snorted. I smiled sheepishly.

"I'm sorry. That wasn't polite." Turning around, I marched back to the cushion and flopped back down.

"I didn't mean it exactly the way it sounded. I do not think all those who flirt are unintelligent. Typically, when flirting, it seems a requirement that neither party behaves normally. The girl usually giggles and acts in a way I would consider below her typical intelligence, and the boy acts brasher than usual."

Aryana's teeth flashed at me, white and slightly crooked.

"You have it right, but you're speaking of youths. You're of an age now that you need to consider men. Brashness leaves, and intense cleverness remains. Be yourself. Do not hide your innocence, yet let this man know you are no simple maid to be manipulated."

I nodded slowly.

"The truth is easier than deception," I said in agreement.

"Deception is sometimes needed when truth fails," Aryana said sadly before clearing her expression. "Will you see your father?"

Recalling the baker's message, I gave a reluctant nod.

"Go see Bryn. We will tell him you're here for a visit and send him to you."

Ila accompanied me to the door and wished me luck. I would need luck and patience to deal with the beast while I played this game.

When I reached Father's home, Bryn surprised me by yanking the door open before I reached it. She wore a dazzling smile. Taking my hand, she pulled me inside and revealed with barely concealed excitement that she would be engaged in just a few short days.

"The baker's son?" I asked, happy for her.

She nodded and hugged me tight.

"Then I have the perfect gift for you." I pulled back and dug the blunt silver from my bag.

Her eyes watered as she took the coin with heartfelt thanks.

"His father will host a dinner for us, just a few of the more prominent merchants. I have Father's newest shirt laundered for the occasion. Blye helped sew me a new dress so I'll look like I belong, but I worry about Father. Perhaps, I can use some of this for a new coat."

My smile congealed, not that she noticed.

"It shouldn't matter how one looks, but how one behaves. Father is an educated, well-spoken man."

"Of course," she agreed, tucking the coin into the pocket of her skirt. "It would be wiser to tuck this away in case there is a future need."

"I thought you wanted it for food," I said, trying to keep the exasperation from my voice.

"A week ago, I did. But I'll be married soon and will have plenty of food," she reminded me with a satisfied smile.

Biting my tongue, I said nothing about Father's need for food as I listened to her plans for the future and her dreams of socializing with the other merchant's wives. Father's arrival saved me from the complete history of each family invited to the dinner.

"Benella, I was beginning to worry," he said, hugging me. "Are you well?"

"Yes. But I do have some disturbing news. I saw the baker earlier, and he said he had business to discuss with you and to expect him for dinner in two days." We sat at the table together and Bryn moved to her room, not interested in our conversation. "His manner led me to believe he wanted to discuss me again, but I didn't mention I would not be here."

"I'll tell him you're employed elsewhere if I must, but I hope he won't be so direct." He looked down at his hands. "Does the beast treat you well?"

"Yes." I wanted to say more, like that I didn't need to clean or that I could eat until I burst, but knew Father would then wonder what I did there. So I settled for a plea.

"Please don't worry about me."

"I would be a poor Father if I did not," he said.

SWIFTLY WHINNIED with relief when I fetched him from the livery. He knelt so I could mount, then rose gracefully once I clutched his mane securely. Without needing guidance, he left the livery and picked his way through the market, turning us in the correct direction.

The sun had not yet crested the sky when we neared the estate. Swiftly's ears flicked with increasing frequency as we approached the final bend in the road, where he just stopped moving. I scanned the trees and hoped it wasn't Tennen who Swiftly sensed.

From the trees stepped an old woman. She wore a worn, patched gown and shuffled forward with her focus on the path. She leaned heavily on her staff for each small, mincing step and appeared not to notice us as she changed her course to follow the road toward us.

Watching her painfully slow progress, I knew I had to offer assistance. I slid from Swiftly and patted him when his flank quivered. His reaction seemed odd given how old and fragile the woman appeared. As an enchanted horse, I knew he possessed higher reasoning and wondered what about the woman worried him. Perhaps, because of his enchanted state, he didn't like strangers.

"Hello," I called.

The woman stopped her forward shuffle to look up at me. She looked vaguely familiar.

"Are you going to Water-On-The-Bridge?" I asked.

Her watery blue eyes stared at me, but she made no reply.

"It's a long way on foot," I said slowly, wondering if her hearing might be the problem. "Do you need assistance?"

Her sudden cackling laughter made me jump and Swiftly scream in terror. He bolted down the road, veering toward the trees opposite the estate to avoid her. Tendrils of fear wove through my veins and pooled in my stomach.

"We don't have much time," the old woman said.

I recognized her voice when she spoke but couldn't place it.

"Have we met?"

"Twice, but never officially," she said and started forward. This time her steps were not mincing; she strode toward me with an easy gait that did not match her apparent age.

"I'm Rose. Let us talk." She had a wild look in her eyes as she reached for me.

When her hand gripped my shoulder, the road disappeared; and we stood in the familiar room of her cottage. Having been in it once before, even befuddled, I would not forget it. My gaze wanted to wander the peculiar objects hanging from her walls, but I forced it to remain on her as she moved to sit in one of the room's matching chairs. She motioned for me to sit as well. The thick furs that draped the wooden frames provided a comfortable amount of cushion.

"You think to free him?" she asked bluntly.

I knew she meant the beast.

"I only seek to help him."

"If you want to help him, leave him as he is. He is better for it."

"Better?" I found that hard to believe. He was volatile as the beast, chafing at the loss of his true self.

"Without a doubt. Did he tell you everything?"

I eyed her for a moment and decided to speak as bluntly as she had.

"Hardly. He told me that you cast a spell on him, one he could win free of if he gives you one night of pleasure. I've determined a few other pieces on my own."

"Oh?" she said with a contemptuously raised brow.

"He was once human and, I believe, the Liege Lord. And he wasn't the only one affected by the spell you cast. I believe some of the other creatures here were once human as well."

"So wise," she said. "Have you determined why I cast my spell?"

I shook my head and remained silent, sensing her building anger.

"He was a man focused only on his baser needs. He

105

drank when thirsty, slept when tired, and fucked when aroused, which was often. He ignored his responsibilities as Liege Lord completely. This area was overrun with thieves of all sorts and impoverished by his assumed entitlements. He turned a blind eye to the problems of the people who looked to him for protection and guidance. He even went so far as to appoint a Head that organized the thieves instead of ousting them. Had I not stepped in and cut the head from the snake, it would have consumed the north. For the safety of the people, he cannot return to power."

Her explanation was certainly compelling, but her requirement of him to win back his freedom bothered me.

"If you opposed his fornication, why require it for him to win back his freedom?" I asked.

"Why not? It should be easy for him, a man who would put his stick in anything. And, what a fine stick he has. Why not use it on me? He tried valiantly in the beginning, plowing into me until I was raw with it. I lay there willingly, yet, I wonder how many he took who were not so willing."

I felt ill, but Rose just laughed again, a low menacing sound.

Outside the cottage, the beast's roar filled the air. She snickered.

"He has learned a few tricks over the years and may eventually prove not entirely useless," she said. "Listen closely. I've trained him. When I first cast him to his true form, a beast, he would barge in here whenever his cock stood straight, thinking he would finally be free of me. Now…" she trailed off and glanced at the door with a small smile.

After a moment of silence, a fist banged on the door hard enough to rattle the hinges. I glanced at Rose. Her smile widened, and she winked at me.

"Enter."

The door eased open when I would have expected a crash.

"Rose," the beast growled, ducking through the door. "Why have you taken her?"

"I thought she and I should have a proper chat," she said, standing. "She had a few misconceptions of you, and I wanted to set them straight. Have you checked on Egrit, today? She can almost walk normally again."

My eyes widened as I realized she spoke of the wood nymph. Had he approached her again in my absence?

"Come," he said, holding out a hand to me.

My gaze lingered on his clawed paw then drifted to his face. He wasn't asking. He was commanding.

"Remember what I told you," Rose said as I touched my hand to his.

CHAPTER SIX

THE BEAST LED ME FROM THE COTTAGE, KEEPING A FIRM hold on my hand until we reached the manor. My mind spun with so many observations and questions that I didn't notice the distance or time that passed. I'd already guessed the beast was once the Liege Lord, and the candle maker had told a brief bit of his history. A history I hadn't fully believed. Could I be certain I knew it now? Stories often differed depending on the view of the speaker. I wouldn't call the beast kind, exactly, but I did think he had the capacity for fair judgment. After all, he'd remained consistent with his punishment for trespassing...until me. He never truly harmed children. A bruise on the butt, at most, when they landed after being tossed. I'd witnessed worse in parental discipline. And as for women, I wanted to say he was kind to them too, but the wood nymph hadn't received kind treatment.

Rose's statement about the beast forcing his attention twisted my stomach, though; and I tried to distance myself from the problem so I could see it clearly. Facts. Observations. I needed to focus on those.

The beast had been a poor, perhaps horrible, liege lord. Therefore, the enchantress had improved the lives of the villagers dependent on the estate by casting her spell upon him. The candle maker confirmed both points, though he hadn't mentioned Rose.

I frowned, having noticed we walked the hallway to the library. Inside, the beast had another game ready for us.

"I need to think," I said, too confused to sit with him. Then I fled.

In my room, I paced. Rose's chief complaint had been his rule, but too much of our discussion had been on his lust. She claimed to be here to protect the people, but what of the baker and his manipulations? What of Tennen and Splane's unfair treatment of me?

If I'd been an enchantress angry at a liege lord for the poor care of his people, I would have made him suffer the same fates they'd been forced to endure. Fear of violence, rape, hunger...I imagined that over fifty years ago the villagers had experienced all of that with thieves populating these woods. Yet, she had put the beast in the estate, had given him power to protect and heal himself, an endless supply of food, and a tempting wood nymph upon which he could force himself. The only actual punishments, from my viewpoint, were the change in his form and having to fornicate with Rose.

None of it made sense, and it seemed to me that Rose played her own game. She not only punished him with a change in form but many others along with him. I felt certain the crow, wood nymphs, tree, and Swiftly had all been humans. What were their crimes?

I stopped my pacing and stared vacantly out the window.

The tree had asked me to teach the beast. When I'd reflected on what the beast might need to learn, I'd thought kindness, patience, and civility. Perhaps there was more. I cringed at that, though. Three virtues were hard enough to teach. Yet, in one thing, Rose was right: the man who had come before the beast could return to Liege Lord.

Perhaps the tree wanted me to teach him to be a better person. I sighed, unsure how I could help with that when Rose still promoted all of the qualities that made him a poor lord. She complained that he had assumed entitlements. How did giving him such vast magical control over the estate teach him humility?

Frustrated with the beast, Rose, and the tree, I wanted to reach up and yank at my own hair. Why couldn't people just say what they meant? The whole thing felt like a deception.

Aryana's words sprang to mind. Deception is sometimes needed when truth fails. What truth failed fifty years ago?

"Benella?" the beast spoke quietly from behind me, bringing me back to the present. Light no longer shone through the window. The night sky sparkled with stars.

"I know exactly where I am, but have never felt so lost," I said, turning to look at him.

"What did she tell you?" he asked.

He stood just within my door, still dressed in trousers and standing on two legs. The mist pooled around his feet, ready to cover him if he needed it, but I saw his worried expression clearly.

How could a beast, a true beast, show such concern? Such uncertainty? It settled my mind. I would play a game of my own, a dangerous one that might earn the retribution of an angry enchantress, the wrath of a volatile beast, and the scorn of my family. No matter the ending, I would be the one to suffer. But my suffering could free a beast, who might not deserve it, and his servants, who most likely did deserve it.

"She told me what she thought would stop me from helping you," I said honestly. "But it doesn't matter. I will still try to help you."

He exhaled slowly, showing his relief. His reaction helped reassure me that I was making the right choice.

"We will keep going as we have, and eventually, if you hold to your word not to expend your energies on anyone other than Rose, you will be able to do what you must."

Now, I just needed to keep his hope of freedom alive while preventing him from breaking the curse until he learned how to be a better person in order to rule properly. The impossibility of the task was not lost on me.

THE BEAST WAITED outside my door the next morning.

"Let's work in the kitchen again today," I said and led the way without waiting for his answer.

He followed me quietly while I considered my plan.

I'd already shown him the pride that came from working with one's own hands, thanks to the bet about making breakfast. I planned to continue on that theme. Yet, I knew he would tire of cooking unless there was some type of reward to inspire him. Rewards always seemed to help promote the desired behavior. After all, Father kept his class quiet with the promise of earlier dismissal, and Bryn had taught the goat to hold still for milking by giving her carrots. I felt certain I could do something similar with the beast. Yet, I needed to have care about what I offered as a reward. I considered my options carefully and decided, sometimes, praise was enough of a reward. I would start with that.

In the kitchen, we used the chef's books to make an elaborate breakfast, which we didn't eat until closer to lunch. Covered in flour, a splattering of eggs, and some other unknown smears, I sat at the table with a sigh. The beast had willingly assisted the entire time and didn't look any cleaner.

"I will never again take for granted Bryn's skill in the kitchen," I said, eyeing the table.

The food before us looked questionable. The book had listed several different versions of an egg tartlet. According to the chef's writing, the egg would cause the mixture to raise high above the crust. Ours clung to the bottom of a very dark, stiff crust.

"I thought all women learned to cook," he said, poking at the egg.

"Perhaps most do. I wanted to learn my letters and numbers instead," I said. "I found there were many more interesting puzzles I could solve that way. Finding solutions is like winning a game, and it gives me an immense satisfaction. If I can't read, then I'd rather be outside, not in the kitchen, or worse, sewing."

Bravely, I tried to cut into the tartlet. I sawed back and forth to force the blade through the egg. Having won a slice free, I offered it politely to the beast.

"What were your favorite pastimes?" I asked, keeping the question to the past so I could watch his eyes as he thought about his past self. Did he like that man? Could he see any of his own faults?

"It's been so long, I don't recall," he replied just before he tried a bite. He grimaced as he chewed, but I didn't pay much attention to that.

I had noted the lie in his eyes. He did recall his pastimes but did not want to admit them to me. Did he find shame in them? I hoped so.

"Then you should try to discover them. Or find new ones. How is it?" I asked after he chewed for several moments.

"Horrible," he said bluntly, setting down the slice.

I laughed, stole his slice so I wouldn't need to saw through the tartlet again, and took a small bite. It tasted fine, but the texture ruined it.

"This isn't bad for a first try. I think we overbaked it or had the flame too high. Let's try again."

We made three more tartlets as the day progressed. The final one passed with both our approvals, though it was far from the fine dishes the beast could magic.

After finishing the last bite, I stood with a sigh. "We better start washing if we want to see our beds yet tonight."

"Wash?" he asked, staring at me in partial dread.

"The pots, pans, spoons, and every surface in here. I think we spattered eggs on the ceiling." I pointed up at a spatter I'd watch fly from the beast's mixing bowl during our first attempt.

"No," he said firmly.

"I understand."

While cooking, his cooperation had been easily gained by asking for his help and praising his efforts. Earning his cooperation for cleaning would require more than a request for assistance and a word of thanks.

I bent and started unlacing my boots. My feet hurt from standing stationary for most of the day, and I wanted to walk barefoot on the cool stone floor. But mostly, I knew how it would look to the beast.

"If you don't want to help, you won't upset me; but I do ask that you leave so you're not in my way." I pulled off one boot then the other. "If you stay, I'll put you to work."

I stood with a stretch and felt his eyes on me as I went to fetch some water. He watched me put it on the fire to warm. Knowing I had his attention, I stood before the flames for a moment and lifted my underskirt to wipe my face, exposing a leg all the way to mid-thigh.

Behind me, the beast's chair scraped against stone as he pushed away from the table. I dropped my skirt back into place. He hadn't moved fast enough to see anything; but without a doubt, he knew he'd missed some sort of view.

"Are you helping?" I asked, turning to arch a brow at him innocently. "If not, you're in my way."

"I will help for a while," he said reluctantly, glancing at my skirts.

I suppressed my triumphant grin.

We cleaned for a long while. When he did something especially helpful, I thanked him and did something innocently to reveal a bit of skin. In my mind, it was nothing he hadn't already viewed when I'd spent the day naked in his presence. But the glimpses seemed to have an even greater effect.

A glimpse of my bare calf when I stood on a chair while trying to wipe the ceiling had him watching me inconspicuously afterward. He always watched me, but his attempt to watch me without being obvious called his regard to even more attention.

When I moved the hot water from the fire, I used my outer skirt to protect my hand and left only my underskirt to cover me. He stood washing the butcher block, and I knew the fire glowed through my skirts and outlined my legs.

"We never addressed the issue of my underclothes," I said, turning toward him innocently. "Do I get them back?" I walked the water to the washtub and waited for his answer.

"They will be there when you need them," he answered hoarsely.

I thanked him and kept working.

For the remainder of the night, I focused on not displaying anything else.

THE UNDERCLOTHES DID NOT REAPPEAR the next morning, and I smiled as I picked out a dress to wear. Another plain one, though the wardrobe kept its usual variety.

Not wanting him to grow bored with any one task, I decreed we would try to discover some of his old pastimes. I knew what a few of those were and honestly did not want him to think about them once again, so I took him to the last place we would find them.

Connected to the library, a door led to the Lord's study. We breached the dusty room on the pretext of looking for clues.

On the desk sat an open ledger. I glanced at it casually when I walked a circle around the small room. Many of the books that lined the shelves were past ledgers or family accounts of daily life. A feminine swirl covered the open pages of the most current ledger. The last number noted had been underscored with force. Thirty-seven gold. An astounding amount to me, but for a vast estate it seemed a bit sparse.

"How many servants used to live here?" I asked, coming back to the study door, leaving the room undisturbed.

"Twenty, at any given time," he said, his eyes following me.

I caught a glimpse of something in their depths, but it disappeared quickly. It made me feel vulnerable, as if he knew my game.

I nodded, acknowledging his answer, but said nothing.

"Have you ever danced, Benella?"

"Yes," I said, wondering why he asked.

"I want to show you something." He reached for my hand and wrapped his fingers around my own.

Frowning at our joined hands, I followed where he led, to a large cavernous room with a polished wood floor. The curtains were pulled back and the windows thrown open. A pair of songbirds perched on the sill of one window and picked up a soft melody, and I added birds to the list of creatures who may have once been human. With a quick sinking dread, I thought of all the traps I'd set near the estate and hoped I'd never accidentally eaten someone.

The beast spun me about and caught me tight to his chest. I tilted my head back to look up at him as he swept me into a twirling dance that swirled my skirts around my legs. My feet skimmed the floor as he guided me through unfamiliar moves. The quick turns he executed made my head spin, and I laughed, which spurred him to twirl me faster. One of his hands rested on my lower back, its heat penetrating my dress until I could barely focus on the dance. I found the sensation...odd. Not disturbing, just different.

During moments like these, I liked the beast most. He seemed playful and earnest and willing to please.

The birds ended their song, and the beast guided me to a halt but did not release me. I looked at him expectantly, still smiling.

"I recall thinking dancing tedious," he said slowly. "A social requirement. I believe I may have misunderstood it. It has so much more potential." A small grin tugged his lips. "Especially when I know my partner isn't wearing her underclothes."

My brows shot up before I could stop myself.

Using the hand not anchored to the small of my back, he reached up and began to untangle my braid, reminding me he was no tame beast.

"What are you doing?"

"It's been a month," he said with a slight purr in his voice. "I can touch you now."

My heart froze and panic claimed me.

"Breathe, Benella," the beast said softly.

"Stop." The word came out strangled, but I found the strength to push against him.

His iron grip tightened for a moment before he withdrew his hands. My release eased my fears a little.

"You will not use me like you did—" I took a calming breath. "If you abuse me, I will leave," I vowed. "And no threat will incite me to return."

The beast scowled at me.

"You have the ability to ruin a perfectly good day," he said.

"How did I ruin it? I wasn't the one contemplating forcing myself on another." I glared back at him.

He growled at me then looked out the window, clearly frustrated but keeping his distance.

"You have Rose if you recall," I said. "Save your attentions for her. I'm only your inspiration."

"You haven't been very inspiring," he replied, referring to his last attempt.

"If I'm too inspiring, people get hurt."

He had the grace to flinch, showing he truly regretted his actions. He needed better control. How could I teach him self-denial, though?

"What is something you find completely uninspiring?" I asked.

He scowled at me and remained silent. I understood his meaning.

"If you can find something that uninspires you, something you can use to calm yourself and prove to me that it works, I will make an effort to be more inspiring."

I left him in the sunlit room.

He absented himself from my presence the remainder of the day and the two days following. I kept myself busy in the library, reading a book I'd found about fishing and the various baits to try depending on the weather and time of day. Occasionally, I would feel as if someone watched me; but when I looked up, no one would be there.

Trays would appear beside me at random times. Looking at the dishes, I knew he had made several of them himself, and I fought not to grin triumphantly. Cooking did not indicate reform, but it did show progress.

ON THE THIRD MORNING, I discovered the garden fully weeded and walked back inside, confused. After that, I began an exploration of the manor and found several things changed. Poorly washed linens hung in the laundry, there was a large supply of firewood in the kitchen, and it smelled as if someone had scrubbed the floor in the main entry.

"Sir?" I called loudly.

The mist rolled along the floor almost immediately.

"What?" The clipped word and his volume spoke his irritation.

"I'm curious what you've been doing these last few days."

He snorted.

"Trying to find something uninspiring."

"Any luck?" I kept any trace of humor from my voice.

"What do you think?"

I ignored his sarcasm.

"Have you tried reviewing the ledgers of past Lords to determine what in that year made the estate profitable and what lost the estate money? I wouldn't start with anything recent. Perhaps two generations back? Look for a pattern and try to determine what you would have done differently."

He didn't reply. Instead, he stalked off, taking his mist with him.

I endured another uneventful day.

THE BEAST WOKE me by barging into my room. He wore trousers and a mostly unbuttoned shirt.

"I'm ready to try again today," he said.

I sat up slowly, letting the covers fall away. The gossamer gown left little to the imagination.

"The ledgers proved uninspiring?" I asked as I lifted the covers off my legs and slid from the bed.

The mist quickly gathered around him.

"Yes."

I went to the wardrobe and picked out another plain gown.

"I'm ready to try again," he repeated as if I'd not heard him.

Smiling over my shoulder, I nodded then turned my attention back to the gowns.

"You may be, but I require proof before prancing about you naked again. Please excuse me while I change," I said calmly. "And no mist today," I added when he moved to leave.

He growled and slammed the door, leaving me to dress.

A few minutes later, I emerged. He paced in the hallway, the mist completely absent.

I smiled in greeting.

"I thought we could play a game in the library."

Not waiting for him, I moved down the hallway toward the library. His heavy footfalls sounded behind me after a moment.

When he saw me move toward the game board, he gave a slight growling groan of frustration.

"I tire of that game."

Sitting on a padded chair, I looked up at him.

"But I do not. Please, sit," I said, my tone more command than invitation.

His lip curled, but he sat. Several minutes into the game, I could sense his impatience boiling and decided it time to distract him. I'd selected the gown with care that morning. Most of the simple, appropriate gowns had two layers in the bodice, a finely woven soft underlay and a coarser overlay. The underlay, typically white, prevented the neckline from gaping if tied properly. I had tied it loosely.

Placing my elbow on the edge of the table, I leaned forward to rest my chin on my hand. After a moment, the beast ceased moving. I waited a heartbeat longer, then moved my piece with a satisfied smile before straightening.

When I looked up, his eyes studied the board intently.

In seven moves, the play had shifted to the far side of the board. I wanted to laugh at his wit. He could have ended the game but played his pieces for another purpose. I gave him what I knew he hoped for and stood slightly, bending at the waist to make my next move. He made a small noise, and I quickly looked up, a true frown on my face.

He met my gaze.

"Sir?" I questioned softly.

"Go eat," he said.

I looked beyond him and saw a tray on the table.

"We will continue afterwards," he said.

Only once I stood and moved away from him did I realize his growl had been missing. When I looked back at him, he was gone. Through the doors to his study, I caught a glimpse of him as he sat at his desk.

I grinned.

THE BED DIPPED, waking me enough that I rolled over. The beast's hand smoothed my hair from my face.

"Sleep," he whispered.

Instead of sinking back to sleep, his voice roused me further. He sounded sad.

"Restless dreams?"

"Yes." He pulled me close to his side with a sigh.

I snuggled in, resting my head on his shoulder, and my hand on his chest. I gently patted him as I fell back to sleep.

I DEBATED over what to wear the next day and decided for normal. I'd tempted him enough with a bit of skin the day before. Today, I would try to tempt him through words.

Twisting my braid, I pinned it up in a knot at the back of my head then opened my door with a smile. The beast waited for me just outside, dressed again in trousers.

"No games today," I promised.

His mouth turned down in a slightly disgruntled expression, and I quickly turned away to hide my smile.

In the kitchen, I set about making breakfast and asked him to help in little ways: starting the fire, fetching a bowl, stirring the eggs. He did it all without complaint. When we sat to eat, I gave him a large portion and thanked him for his help. He said nothing in return. We ate in silence for several moments while I contemplated flirting and the sisters' advice. I struggled to find something to say.

"You're unusually quiet," he said, studying me closely.

"As are you."

He looked back at his food.

Aryana's recommendation to be myself made me want to wrinkle my nose. I decided on an honest compliment.

I reached over and lightly touched his arm.

"I think I'm starting to like living here," I said quickly and sincerely. "Without your growl...well, I like spending time with you."

His gaze bored into mine as if trying to find some hidden meaning.

"Do you?" he asked softly, but his tone hinted at anger.

I tilted my head with a frown.

"Was it wrong of me to tell you so?"

"Why are you telling me?"

My lips twitched at his suspiciousness, but my amusement quickly faded when a rumble started in his chest. I slowly withdrew my touch from his arm.

"How can I expect honesty from you if I cannot give it myself?" I asked, confused at his reaction. Instead of holding his gaze, I looked down and took another bite.

He continued his soft growl as I chewed and swallowed.

"Have you thought of any of your prior pastimes, yet?" I asked, trying to change the subject.

"In fact, I have," he said with a purr.

Before I realized his intent, he pulled me to my feet and sat me in his lap. I didn't react other than to glance at him. For some reason, telling him I liked it here had annoyed him. I didn't understand why but understood that his volatile mood couldn't be trusted. I reached for a misshapen biscuit and pinched off a bite, calmly eating it as if I were sitting in my own chair.

The pastime he'd recalled currently bruised my backside. I wondered what exactly I'd done to cause it. Whatever the issue, I did not intend to remain to see where his current mood led.

I pinched off a larger portion and met his hungry gaze.

"Open your mouth," I said softly.

Surprise lit in his eyes a moment before he did so.

Instead of putting the large bite in his mouth, I shoved in the remainder of the biscuit. He grunted then loosened his hold to cough into his hand. I quickly slid from his lap and stood by my chair, watching him warily as he continued to cough and sputter.

"Are you trying to kill me?"

"Hardly. But I am trying to reason out why I angered you."

He stood with menacing slowness, and I grabbed my plate of cold eggs and threw the contents at him.

"Would you stop throwing your food at me?" he roared.

The frustration in his tone eased some of my fear, and I laughed at my own audacity. His eyes narrowed. I squealed and scrambled for the outer door, barely closing it behind me. Something heavy thudded into it. I sniggered.

"I can still hear you," he bellowed.

He was truly angry, yet something possessed me to laugh again. It was an open challenge, and I took off at a sprint, barefoot through the weeds. Behind me, the door crashed open. I laughed louder and ran faster. A path around to the front of the house opened before me. Behind me, I heard it close and the beast's angry bellow as he tore through it.

"I recall a pastime from *my* childhood," I called, slowing. "I was fairly good at it. Let us see if I still am."

He roared in response, obviously still angry.

Moving forward, I burst into the front yard and onto the gravel drive. The stones bit into the soles of my feet, but I didn't slow. On the other side, the male wood nymph waved to me. I smiled and ran his direction. He pointed the way to another open path.

"Thank you. Warn the others to stay out of his way and to keep the path open, please." He nodded as I ran past.

I ran until I found a large tree right on the path, which I quickly climbed. Seconds later, the beast ran under the limbs, and I grinned at the egg that still clung to his fur.

I jumped from the tree and ran back the way I'd come. The nymph was nowhere in sight. I ran up the steps to the manor, eased open the door, and slipped inside. I didn't slow as I sprinted up the steps to my room or when I opened the doors to his room. I closed everything behind me before diving under his bed.

Long minutes passed. His roar from outside rattled the pane, and I began to doubt the wisdom of my impromptu game. There hadn't been any wisdom. I'd done something completely outrageous to distract him from his arousal. And where did that leave me? Under his bed. Just as I thought to creep out and find a safer place, the door to my room slammed open. I heard fabric ripping and furniture crashing. I trembled, regretting my spontaneity.

The door to his room flew open, and I held my breath. I heard him move around the room. I didn't try to look and follow his progress. I held completely still.

Suddenly, his hands closed around my ankles, and he yanked me from under the bed. I stared up in shock at the beast's face, which hovered just inches from my own.

"Found you," he purred.

"That's because you cheated," I said in a rush, unsure of his mood. "You didn't count the proper amount of time."

We stayed still, gazing at each other. So many emotions flitted through his gaze that I couldn't even begin to speculate their meaning.

"Go," he said suddenly, pushing away from me. "Leave me in peace."

Without hesitation, I quickly scurried to my own room. As soon as the doors closed, a thundering crash came from his side.

I'd thought to flirt with him but had only done so with honest praise. I stared at the doors wondering what had gone wrong.

CHAPTER SEVEN

AFTER TWO DAYS OF QUIET AVOIDANCE—ON HIS PART, NOT mine—I finally found him in the kitchen, waiting near a set table. I approached cautiously and stopped a good distance away.

"Sit," he commanded. "Eat."

"No, thank you," I said softly.

He grunted in frustration but did not growl.

"Why not?"

"I seem to upset you no matter what I do or say. Then you upset me, and suddenly you're wearing more of my food."

He snorted and studied me for a moment.

"A bribe then? What price do you ask to sit and eat with me?"

"A full meal without any food decorating your fur?"

He nodded with a slight smile curving his lips.

"Answers," I said.

"To what questions?"

"I'm not yet sure. All I ask is your calm honesty. Instead of stating something isn't my concern, tell me why you do not want to answer the question."

I moved toward the table, knowing he would do as I asked.

"Why did my statement about liking it here upset you?"

"I thought it a lie."

"You no longer do?"

"No."

"Why not?"

He sighed gustily and pushed back his plate.

"Because...of so many reasons."

I took a bite and waited. He didn't disappoint.

"You don't hold back what you're thinking. And, you are willingly risking my anger to speak truthfully. Though I've given you enough cause to leave, you haven't yet done so. You do not act resentfully toward me, nor do you make outrageous or selfish demands when given the opportunity. What else can I think, but that you really do like it here, with me," he said softly.

I smiled widely at him.

"Well, there aren't many places I can go about my day naked," I teased. "Perhaps that is the draw."

He gave a half laugh and started eating. I dared to hope

we were actually becoming friends. I reached for a covered plate to see what else he'd made.

"Wait, it's—"

Too late, I touched the hot dome and burned two fingers. I hissed in pain. The beast moved quickly to my side, kneeling by my chair.

"Let me see." Not waiting for me to move, he reached for my hand.

The tips of my fingers pulsed red. He brought them to his mouth, his tongue flicking out to swipe at the pads. My heart gave an odd flutter as my chest tightened. He licked the pads again, taking with him more of the sting. Heat crawled up my neck, and a strange warmth started in my middle. I frowned at him.

"Thank you," I said pulling my hand free. "They feel much better."

His gaze held me, and he slowly nodded, an unknown emotion lighting his eyes.

What did he see when he looked at me?

AFTER DRESSING in a plain dress for the day, I led the beast on a walk to visit the old tree that had spoken to me twice.

"What was your life like here before Rose enchanted everything?" I asked, sitting on the bank of the pond.

"I honestly don't recall the details. I drank fine wines

and liquors, entertained many guests, played games. Why do you ask?"

"What of your family?" I removed my slippers then pulled up my skirts before stepping into the water. It chilled my skin.

"My father died long before Rose enchanted me. My mother...she left not long before Rose came." He cleared his throat. "Mother was ill and went south looking for help. She died years ago."

"You're alone."

"I was," he said.

My stomach grew warm at his sentiment.

"How deep is this water?" I asked, changing the subject.

"Not at all. Why?"

I grinned at him, waded a few feet out, then kicked water, hitting him fully in his face. He sputtered indignantly for a moment before chasing me into the water in a cascading splash that thoroughly soaked me.

Scooping more water to splash at him, I waged war. His splashes far surpassed mine for the next several minutes.

"I yield," I called, finally.

His matted, wet fur clung to him, and I shivered under my waterlogged dress.

"Would you kindly have a hot bath waiting for me in my room?" I asked with a stutter.

"Of course," he said, leading me to the front door. A trail of water marked our progress as we made our way to

our rooms. He left me at my door with a bow and went to
his own suite.

A large tub waited for me, steam rising from the water.
I gladly peeled off the dress and sank into its depth with a
sigh. Not a moment later, the door behind me clicked open
then closed again.

"Do you mean to watch me bathe?" I asked, resisting
the urge to turn around.

"I do," he answered softly.

I felt a twinge of pity for him. He meant to face Rose
again. I nodded and submerged myself, rewetting my hair.

Bravely, I shifted to my knees, counting on his restraint.
My top half cooled in the air as I reached for the soap.
Closing my eyes, I lathered my hair, arms over my head. A
soft noise on the carpet gave away his move to see more.

Blaming my trembling on the cool air, I rinsed my hair
then started soaping the parts of me still out of water.
Curiously, my nipples hardened when my palms passed
over them. A tingle shot from my breast to my pelvis. I
repeated the motion, analyzing my reaction. I'd washed
myself before. Why was this time different?

A blush of pleasure warmed my face, and I rinsed the
soap away, aware of my audience. When I opened my eyes,
he did not stand before me.

Behind me, the door once again clicked open and
closed.

"Good luck," I whispered in the empty room before
finishing my bath.

I FELT him lay on the bed beside me at some point during the night. I rolled toward him and laid a hand on his chest, feeling the fur.

"What happened?" I murmured in sleepy disappointment.

"When I closed my eyes I pictured you but..." He sighed. "It wasn't enough."

Reaching up, I stroked my fingers along his shoulder.

"We will try again," I promised before giving into sleep once more.

I RODE to the Water just as the sun crested the horizon. Two gold coins rested in my pocket, a gift from the beast. This time I didn't bother with the stables, but rode straight to the Sisters' house. The guard at the back door nodded to me when I dismounted and tied Swiftly to the tree.

"Not a word of this," I whispered to the creature.

Swiftly nickered softly, his eyes on the house. In the shadows behind the guard, I saw a very naked Ila waiting for me.

"If you're good, I'll invite her to take you for a ride. She doesn't wear any underthings either," I said with a light laugh. He made an odd non-horse noise and shook his head as I walked away.

"We've been waiting for you to return," Ila whispered as she wrapped her arms around me in a warm embrace.

"I should have come sooner, but my master demands so much of my time."

"Things are well?"

"Yes. But I do have a purpose for my visit."

"Come, let us bathe."

I nodded and followed her down the steps.

Aryana did not wait in the tubs as usual, but Ila didn't seem surprised by it.

"I'd grown so used to Aryana down here that it's odd without her," I said as we walked through to the back room.

"She is still sleeping," Ila said.

As she helped me rinse, I broached one of the subjects on my mind.

"My master gifted me with some coin, and I had hoped to purchase some of the oil you used in my hair. I like the smell of it."

"Of course," she said as she poured water over me to rinse the soap away. "I make it myself."

"It's lovely."

Ila laughed lightly.

"I will make a new scent just for you."

I thanked her as we dried.

"I have another question," I said after a few moments of quiet. "You've explained pent energies. I'm wondering if a woman could have pent energies, too."

I'd watched their demonstration with Gen, and after my interaction with the beast, I deduced sight and touch of a woman and her body contributes to a man's energies. But would the same work for a woman? The beast had alluded that it was possible. But, if so, did the beast have the knowledge to try and build the enchantress's energies? I thought that might be the crux of the problem in achieving a full night of pleasure. The beast was certainly able to find his pleasure but could he find hers?

Ila smiled at me.

"Yes, we can. Though, we don't become angry like men do when it occurs."

"How do a woman's energies become pent?" I wanted to help the beast, but part of me was plain curious after his remark.

Ila made a slight coughing sound.

"Perhaps we can discuss this when you came back for the oil? I should have it ready by midday. It should give you time to visit your sister."

Reluctantly, I agreed and went to visit with Bryn.

Bryn excitedly spoke of all the people she'd met now that she'd engaged herself to the baker's son. She gushed about how the baker himself treated her as a daughter and often took her on a tour of the bakery to explain the business further.

I tried to ask about the babe, but it seemed to upset her otherwise bubbly mood so I quickly asked about the wedding again. She spoke of her wedding feast guest list and Blye's growing success as a dressmaker.

"She wanted me to ask if you could find her some more embellishments for hats or if you might have more of that thread," she finally finished.

"I'll see what I can do," I promised, standing to leave.

I walked Swiftly back to the Sisters. Ila again met me at the door and handed me a vial the size of my palm.

"You don't need to use much. Apply it when your hair is wet, and comb it through."

I grinned at her and gave her the two gold coins.

"This is too much," she said with a rough gasp.

"An advance for the next order. Please give anything that remains to my father." She seemed mollified by that.

"Do you have a moment to speak?" I asked, hoping she still might explain how a woman's energies become pent. Her appearance at the door, and the fact that they now had customers made it unlikely.

Ila glanced to her right, and Aryana stepped into view.

"We need to leave some mystery for you to discover on your own," Ila said. "If we reveal all of the secrets of seduction, it takes the magic from the moment."

"Seduction?" I tested the word, trying to recall a meaning.

"Not something generally discussed in polite company. The art of persuasion in which the end result is..." Ila looked to Aryana.

"I believe fornication would be the best word choice with our Benella."

Neither would say any more. With nothing further to discuss, I left.

WHEN I RETURNED to the manor, in my frustration, I slammed the door to the kitchen.

"This is unusual," the beast said as he entered the room. "What vexes you so?"

"Have you ever heard of the Whispering Sisters?" I asked.

"Yes, but why have *you* heard of them?"

"It is where my father teaches. And, I've made a few friends there. At least, I thought they were friends." I sat heavily on a chair. "They've been an invaluable source for information. There are things they know that have helped me understand—"

"You've been receiving advice from whores?"

His sudden upset surprised me.

"There is no need to yell. How else am I to learn about these things? Men are complex creatures on their own. Throw an enchantment on one, and he is impossible."

He took a slow, deep breath, and I waited for him to calm.

"Why are you upset with them?" he asked.

"As I mentioned, they've been open with their advice. Until today."

"What did you ask today?"

"How do a woman's energies become pent? I understand fucking, as you put it, but don't understand where the appeal is for the woman."

He made a choked noise and immediately left the room.

"That's about the reaction they had," I yelled after him. "I don't think it fair that everyone is keeping this knowledge to themselves."

Really, how was I supposed to help him when I didn't know?

CHAPTER EIGHT

I STARED INTO THE DARKNESS LONG AFTER I BLEW OUT MY candle.

"Benella," the beast whispered nearby, startling me. "Would you like to understand how a woman's energies become pent?"

"Yes," I said with frustration. I didn't see how he could accurately enlighten me, though, given his lack of success with Rose.

"It will take time," he said. "Several days perhaps. And I cannot tell you, I must show you."

Ah. So perhaps his lack of success with Rose wasn't due to his understanding but his technique. Showing would be beneficial.

"And I will need to touch you. With no restrictions."

I didn't like the sound of that.

"No fornication," I warned.

"No, Benella," he said with a softly amused calm.

"You have my permission, then," I said, very curious as to what exactly he would do. "But only on the condition that you will stop whenever I tell you."

He lay next to me and pulled me close like he'd done so many times before.

"Agreed. Now, sleep," he whispered, the furred tips of his fingers stroking the skin of my arm. It felt so good, my eyes soon drifted closed.

During the night, I woke to his touch on my bare stomach. It remained feather light, but insistent. It traced a pattern skimming the bottom side of my right breast before dipping and barely brushing the curls between my legs.

I frowned, worried. His erection pressed into my backside.

"Relax," he whispered, moving his touch back to my arm where it caused less concern. Again, he lulled me to sleep.

In the morning, I woke next to him, my gown gone. His hands roamed over my stomach and arms. A burst of heat ignited in my stomach when his fingers brushed over a breast, just missing the nipple.

"Good morning," he said.

"Good morning," I returned, uncomfortable and ready to ask him to stop. But he stood without me asking.

His eyes ran the length of me, and my heart stuttered.

"I'll leave you to dress," he said.

With a slight grin on his lips, he walked to his room and closed the connecting doors.

I lay there for a moment, stunned. He'd touched me and walked away. His control relieved me. Yet, if that was an example of how he attempted to build Rose's energies, no wonder it didn't work.

Dressed in trousers and a shirt, I met him in the hallway.

"Interesting choice of clothes. What do you have in mind today?"

"I thought we might fish again."

"Lead on," he said willingly.

Remembering my comment from the last time we left the safety of the walls, he offered to toss me over the wall, which I quickly accepted. My stomach churned in delight as I sailed through the air. I landed with a light bounce in the vine net. Once it released me, the beast landed softly by my side.

At the river, I rolled up my pant legs, dangled my feet in the water, and sat back to think. The beast's skills were lacking and the Sisters wouldn't help me. I didn't have many other options to try to help him. Bryn would ask too many questions if I approached her, and I wasn't sure if Blye had the experience.

"You're very quiet," he said from beside me.

"I'm trying to determine our next course," I replied distractedly.

Did I dare speak with Rose to find out where he was

lacking? She'd spoken very frankly regarding his efforts before. But what if asking upset her? Would I then end up as a beast, too? Not a very pleasant prospect. Speaking to her would be my last, dire resort.

"What do you mean?"

"To help you last a full night with Rose. I'd thought perhaps if we could improve your skill at building a woman's pent energies, we might succeed the next time, but I'm not knowledgeable—"

"Improve my skill?" he sputtered indignantly.

"Well, last night, you didn't inspire—"

"It was not supposed to." His exasperation was obvious.

"Then what was the purpose?"

"Did you fear me touching you this morning?"

I shook my head. Even naked I hadn't been afraid, just uncertain.

"Did you feel anything just before I left?"

The way he watched me had me wondering if he knew.

"A bit of warmth in my middle, but nothing lingering after I dressed for the day."

He reached over, plucked the pole from my hands, and set it out of the way. Then, he gently pushed me back so I lay on the bank. I calmly let him have his way, until he slowly began unbuttoning my shirt.

"Sir?"

"Shh. I want to prove a point and mean you no harm."

I wrinkled my nose, which made him smile, but he

didn't stop. With my bindings exposed, he traced his fingers over my stomach again.

"So the warmth was here?"

My heart gave an odd flip again as I nodded.

"What exactly caused it?"

I blushed scarlet and quickly sat up.

"I'd rather not discuss this. I think my approach was misguided. Even if I had the knowledge, I don't think I could impart it without...well, doing this." I waved a hand at my flushed face. "Have you ever considered visiting the Sisters? Perhaps they would be willing to—"

He barked out a laugh. "An intriguing idea. But you're here now and can tell me what exactly I did wrong." He tugged on my shirt, encouraging me to lie back down.

I cleared my throat and attempted to ignore my heated face.

"I wouldn't say there was a wrong action. Nothing disturbed me or frightened me. Neither did anything inspire me," I said, using his words.

"I see. Please consider giving me another chance," he said softly, his fingers once again trailing my stomach.

"Honestly, I don't see how that will help. You have had fifty years of trying," I said softly and without censure.

"But if you're willing to tell me the effects of what I am trying, I can adjust my technique. Improve perhaps?"

Something about the look in his eyes made me nervous.

"And you will stop when I say?"

"Of course," he assured me.

I hesitantly nodded my agreement, and his grin widened.

"Close your eyes," he commanded, then softly added, "please."

In the obscurity behind my eyelids, I waited for something, unsure what to expect. What he gave was the same touch on my stomach as before. A slow swirl of his fingers over my skin. A circle that slowly expanded, until it almost touched the underside of my breast.

It grew warmer outside.

On the next pass, his fingers teased the edge of my bindings. My nipple tingled, and I found it difficult to breathe normally. His fingers left my skin. When I heard him sit up, I blinked in confusion. He reappeared above me a moment later, holding the pole.

"You have a fish on the line," he said, handing it to me.

A fish? I took a calming breath. My skin tingled from his touch. As I pulled the line in, I saw my error. He had lulled me and was slowly building a tension within me. His declaration for a few days now made sense. He would take his time pulling me further and further into a world I did not yet understand until...fornication. Of course. The beast. I scowled.

I strung the fish onto the line of another shorter pole and stuck the pole into the bank so the fish trailed in the water. My hands drifted to the buttons. His hands reached around me, closing over mine.

"Not yet," his rough voice tickled my ear.

"I would like to stop now." I moved his hands away and buttoned quickly.

He bowed his head at me and said nothing, staying close.

I caught another fish, and ready to leave his quiet, watchful presence, I declared our time outdoors complete.

AFTER CROSSING the wall and walking through the fields and hills, we came to the border of trees on the east side of the manor. Just at their edge, I caught movement. I stopped walking and watched the nymphs, unwilling to disturb a playful moment.

"I'm glad he forgave her," I commented as the nymphs chased each other.

"Forgave her?" the beast asked quietly.

"The first day I read to you and you dallied with her, he refused to talk to her afterward."

The beast's brow furrowed as he watched them as well.

"She looks well," I added softly, studying him instead of the nymphs.

"Yes. Quite," he said and turned away.

When I looked at the nymphs, she was again on her knees in front of her companion, his wooden penis in her mouth. I wondered how exactly that worked for trees.

Then I wondered if the baker would like the taste of her sap.

"Must you study them?" the beast said with impatience, already a distance from me.

I hurried to catch up with him.

A SOFT TOUCH on my thigh woke me in the night. My skin felt hot and sensitive, uncomfortable, and my heart thundered in my chest.

I sat up abruptly, again naked.

"Stop."

His hand fell away as I turned to look at him. He lay beside me, watching me closely. I had the absurd urge to roll toward him and wrap my arms around him.

"What are you doing?" I demanded.

"Touching you."

He looked calm, but even the pants he wore couldn't hide his massive erection. Unknowingly, I'd started a dangerous game with his control. If he could not control himself, I would be the one broken and bleeding like the nymph.

"When I suggested it might be your approach, I didn't understand. Now, I have a better idea what continuing with this means for me. And it frightens me. I do not want to end up like the wood nymph. I do not want to be used and forgotten. Though you might not treat me as a whore, you would treat me as a body with no head attached. Have you given thought to how the pursuit of your game will make me feel?" I spoke softly, hoping to reason with him without angering him.

He leaned in.

"I hurt you once. I will not hurt you again. I swear."

"I'm glad we agree. Please leave."

He snorted.

"I think not," he said.

He reached forward, his fingers skimming my thigh again, first the outside, then the inside. He was just inches from where they met in the middle, his touch causing a slow burn. I desperately wanted to pull him closer, and that yearning scared me.

I scooted from the bed, grabbed a pillow, and dashed across the room. He stood but too slow. I quickly slipped into his room and locked the door. Then just as quickly, I locked the door coming from the hall.

He tried both calmly at first. When he understood that I'd locked him out, he pounded on the adjoining doors.

Raiding his wardrobe, I covered myself with one of his shirts then sat on his bed.

The pounding turned to rage. He didn't yell at me, only growled and slashed at the other side of the wood panels.

The urge to appeal to him, to calm him, held me fiercely. I hated hearing him so upset. Yet, I knew if I opened those doors, he would try to continue with what he had started. So, I remained on the bed, holding my pillow to my chest as I watched for a hint of the rising sun while listening as he tried to tear his way through. The doors held all night, repairing themselves before he could completely breach them.

With the sun, his racket quieted. I sat on his mattress, tired and wondering what to do. After several minutes, I eased from the bed and tiptoed to the doors leading to my room. I leaned my ear to the panel but heard nothing. I tried the handle. It turned, and I cautiously opened the door.

The other side of the wood panel was a patchwork of deep and numerous gouges. It was clear that very little material had separated me from the beast. As I stared, tiny wood fibers moved to mend themselves. If not for the magic of this place, he would have easily ripped his way through the wood. His temper was a frightening thing.

My room was littered with broken furniture and shredded dresses. I felt completely relieved that I'd put on one of his shirts. Nothing in my room remained for me to wear.

My stomach rumbled. Risking running into him and his anger, I tiptoed to the door that led to the hall and eased it open.

He paced in the hallway on all fours, an angry black swirling mist at his feet. Any semblance of the man he'd been during the night was gone. His head whipped toward me.

Before I could move, the mist enveloped me. Sightless, I groped for the door. Instead of the door, I touched fur.

I turned and tried to run, but he caught me up into his arms and started walking with me. I didn't try to struggle.

"You're still angry," I said nervously.

"Very," he growled.

"What do you intend to do?"

"Feed you."

He set me down on the lounge in the library. The mists receded from me while he continued to remain hidden. A food-laden tray sat on the low table.

"Eat," he ordered.

I nibbled at some food as I watched the mist pace back and forth with him. He moved to the shelves, and the rasp of a book sliding from its place made me curious.

"Eat," he said again.

I quickly took another bite of a tartlet while trying to determine his mood. Obviously angry, but driven, too. He had a goal in mind, but what? Light burst from the fireplace as flames suddenly appeared. He growled, and I finished the tartlet in two more bites.

"Drink," he said in a slightly calmer voice.

The cold spring water had barely touched my tongue when a book landed on the cushion next to me.

"Read," he said softly. It was less of a command and more of a plea.

The sudden shift in his mood made me suspicious. He moved behind me and lightly tugged on my braid to undo my hasty work. My eyes drifted to the book. The Medicinal Properties of Flora in the North.

My interest piqued, I picked up the book and read as his fingers trailed through my hair.

I woke with his fingers roaming my body. The mist surrounded me so I couldn't see a thing. His touch was completely unobstructed by the shirt I had been wearing. Heat flooded me. I'd fallen asleep reading. Warm, full, tired, and lulled by his fingers running through my hair, I hadn't had a chance.

The pad of his finger roamed over one nipple, and I gasped at the tingling sensation that spread down between my legs.

Opening my mouth to protest, he surprised me by covering it.

"Quiet and listen," he said, still touching me, fueling a fire that burned me from the inside. "You demanded I consider how my *game* would make you feel."

His finger crossed over my nipple again followed closely by his tongue. The tingling sensations spreading between my legs consumed me. He laved the tender peak for a moment while I panted for breath.

"I have considered it. Have you? How does this make you feel?"

Stretching out my hands, I curled my fingers in his hair

and pulled him back down to my breast. He obligingly sucked it again, the scrape of his fangs adding to the pleasure. The heat spread out slowly, causing an ache in the other breast.

Finally, I understood why Bryn had lain with Tennen. Bryn. Pregnant and rejected. The realization of how this could end for me cooled the heat within me.

I yanked back on his head and sat up.

He growled loudly and pressed me into the back of the lounge. His head dipped to the other breast, giving it the same burning attention. My thoughts jumbled together and instead of pushing his head away, I pulled it closer again.

His hands gripped my legs and started easing the right one over the side of the lounge. His mouth drifted from my breast, and his tongue tickled a trail to my stomach, which dipped and clenched wildly.

With his semi-desertion, a clear thought penetrated the fog in my mind. Sara. The baker. Her crying in shame after he had tasted her.

"Stop!" I cried loudly, startling us both.

He pulled back, but I couldn't see him.

"Did I hurt you?" he asked, obviously confused.

"You selfish, single minded beast," I cried, swinging an arm out and connecting with the side of his head.

He grunted in surprise.

I quickly scrambled off the lounge and out of his reach.

"You *know* what I meant about feelings." My voice

echoed slightly in the room, and I immediately took a slow breath. "You are so focused on you, you would even use the people who are trying to help you. You see something you want and take it regardless of feelings or if it is being given freely. You coerce and bargain to get your way."

The beast growled deep and long.

"No," I said firmly, cutting off his growl. "You are the Liege Lord still, despite your appearance. Remember your responsibility. Remember who you are supposed to be. *That* is why you were enchanted, your complete disregard of your every responsibility and obligation in pursuit of your own satisfaction."

His growl grew, clicking with his anger.

"You know *nothing* of me or my intentions."

The mist cleared the room. The beast was gone.

I let out my pent breath, glad to have escaped. My skin still tingled, and I looked for the shirt. It was gone. Narrowing my eyes, I made my way to my own room. It was neatly restored. The bedding and curtains now a soft green. The white wardrobe stood open and empty. I moved to his room. His wardrobe was also empty.

Sitting on his bed once again, I debated my future.

The progress I'd thought we'd made had evaporated last night with his fit. I'd voiced my concern several times that my presence seemed to make him worse, not better. To be fair, my goal had changed from wanting to free him from his curse to helping him become a better person. The two seemed counterproductive. After all, in his way of thinking, I was in his home to help him please another woman for a full night.

He'd made it clear to me that he expected me to walk around in nothing or next to nothing from the beginning, and I realized he had brought me here to be an object of gratification. I'd bargained for a month of no touching—which had long since passed—thus relegating myself to an object of inspiration. Only I hadn't known that then. Now that I knew what he really wanted from me, could I still help him become a better man?

Groaning, I flopped back on the bed.

Obviously throwing things, yelling, and hitting him didn't work. After his last attempt, I'd thought I could use the hair oil to help him associate a smell with me. Then, he could use that scent when he was with Rose. But before using the hair oil, I'd wanted to be sure he knew the correct way to build her energies. Combined, I'd been so certain it would succeed.

I should have never questioned his knowledge. Questioning it had been like a challenge. He didn't like to be challenged. I groaned again and used a pillow in an attempt to smother myself. It didn't work.

I made this problem. I needed to unmake it and earn back some clothes.

AFTER MAKING a simple meal of cheese, bread, and grapes,

which I'd found in the kitchen, I carried the tray to the library. The doors to his study stood open, drawing my attention.

"Sir?" I called softly holding the tray.

"Go away. You annoy me," he called back flatly. Papers rustled.

I annoyed him? I carried the tray toward the door.

"I wanted to apologize," I said, entering the study. I set the tray on his desk, covering some of the papers he studied. I folded my hands in front of me, waiting for his attention.

"Go away," he repeated, not looking up.

I sighed.

"I shouldn't have questioned your knowledge on a subject of which I'm so obviously ignorant. Not that I want an education," I quickly added.

He still didn't look up.

"I understand why you would take that as a challenge to prove me wrong."

"I was doing nothing of the sort," he said in an exasperated tone.

I studied him as he continued looking at, and switching, papers.

"Doesn't it hurt sitting on your tail?"

"Yes. Will you please leave?"

"Why won't you look at me?"

"Because I will see your natural beauty and will be tempted to continue licking every inch of your skin."

My skin tingled again at the reminder, and I shifted uncomfortably.

"If you don't want me naked, why take all my clothes?"

"I thought your issue with being without clothes was my gaze. If I keep it averted, why clothe you?" he asked reasonably.

"I might catch a chill."

The fire in his study blazed to life.

"I doubt that," he replied.

Stubborn beast. My annoyance over his unwillingness to concede outweighed my amusement at his quick wit.

"What are you looking at?" I asked, determined not to leave until I figured out what game we now played.

"Estate records. Someone once suggested I might find it calming. Go away."

I refrained from stomping my foot.

"What have you found in them?"

"Just as you said. Practices that made the estate profitable. According to records, we sold flowers to candle makers in the south. You wouldn't perchance have seen any during your wanderings?"

"Actually, I have." Still he did not look up.

"I sold them to the candle maker in Konrall."

"There's still a candle maker there?"

"Yes, and a butcher, a smith, a tinker, and a baker. You know nothing of the people closest to your estate?"

Finally, he looked up.

"You've lectured me enough for one day," he said, rising from his chair and walking toward me on two legs.

I stood my ground as his gaze roved over my breasts then went slowly down and back up again. He stood inches from me, his gaze now resting on my pink face.

"Did you learn anything else of interest in the papers?" I asked to distract him.

"Several things, but nothing I'd care to discuss at the moment."

He reached out a finger and trailed the underside of my breast. My skin prickled, and my breast began to ache. His finger drifted over my nipple in a painful yet agreeable way.

"Please stop," I whispered. "I would like one of your shirts."

His hungry expression softened.

"I did not mean to take," he said gently, his hand moving to my face. "You are so beautiful, not just here..." His finger brushed along my jaw, then he leaned in to kiss my forehead. "But here as well."

His lips were thin and hard because of the teeth immediately behind them. Yet, I'd never felt anything more comforting. In that moment, I knew I was losing myself to the beast just as Bryn had lost herself to Tennen. Would I end up rejected, just as she had?

"When you're free," I said quickly, "you will forget me. You can't take everything I am because I need to be me when you're gone."

He pulled back and looked into my eyes, his expression closed off. I waited, bearing his scrutiny, hoping he would understand.

"Thank you for the food, Benella."

I nodded and walked away, feeling his eyes on my backside.

Hopeful, I went to my room, but I still didn't find a shred of clothing. Stubborn man. My stomach rumbled. And he had my food.

CHAPTER NINE

THREE DAYS LATER, I STILL HAD NO CLOTHES; AND THE BEAST continued to avoid me. Instead, he chose to close himself in the study.

Impatient with the stalemate and beyond bored, I sought him out.

"I would like clothes to visit my father."

"Would you mind delaying your visit for a few days, dearest?" he said. "I need to write a few letters and would like you to deliver them for me."

I blinked at him as my heart gave an odd flip. I had expected his refusal but not his explanation or the endearment. His request sounded reasonable, and he'd asked so nicely. With a small sigh, I nodded.

"Could I still have some clothes?"

"When it is time to leave, most certainly," he said distractedly, his eyes devouring the words on the paper.

DECEIT

I struggled for patience.

"The boredom is making me irritable. I would like to walk outside."

"I hardly think walking outdoors naked with all of the servants about is a good idea."

"That's exactly why I need clothes."

"Dearest, I will never get those letters written if you keep distracting me with conversation," he said.

Instead of leaving, I flopped in the chair opposite his desk, sitting sideways with my knees hooked over one arm while leaning back against the other. Although remaining would slow his work and prevent my visit, I couldn't stand the boredom any longer.

"What are the letters about?"

"Estate business." His eyes flicked to me and quickly returned to the papers.

"The estate has business?" I asked with humor.

"It might. If I can finish these letters."

I tipped my head back over the arm of the chair and observed the room upside down.

"If I can't have clothes and occupy myself outside, what else am I to do, but bother you?"

A sudden heat wrapped around my right breast, igniting an increasingly familiar flame in my middle. The suction tugged at an invisible string that led directly between my legs.

Jerking my head up, I saw the beast. He released my nipple with a wet sound and a lick before lifting his head and meeting my wide gaze.

He didn't speak, and I couldn't. We stared at each other in silence for several minutes. Then, he did something completely unexpected.

He closed the distance between us, and pressed his warm lips firmly against mine. But for only a moment. It wasn't a kiss, as in a warm press of soft lips, but a press of skin and teeth. Still, the gesture pierced something inside me. My chest ached with the sweetness of it and the uncertainty in his eyes when he pulled away.

"I'm trying," he said, straightening from me. "But what you did proved too tempting to ignore." He walked back to the desk. "Please find something to do elsewhere."

I sat up as he sat down.

He gave a pained groan.

"Do that again," he begged.

Frowning in confusion, I started to move back into the same position before I realized what I'd done. I'd removed my legs from the arm separately, giving a brief glimpse of the last part of me he had yet to see.

Blood rushed to my face, and I stood stiffly.

"I think I'll go take a bath," I murmured, trying to leave the room with dignity.

"That is not helpful," he said.

My thundering heart didn't return to normal until I stood in the laundry. I started a fire, filled the large kettle, and waited. The door to the outer court called to me, but I had no desire to frolic naked with the nymphs. Then,

DECEIT

inspiration struck. He had removed anything I could use as a cover from his room and my own. Even the curtains tended to disappear if I looked at them too long. But what about the linen closet?

Excited, I ran to the small room and grabbed a clean white sheet from the shelves. Quickly wrapping it around myself, I ran back into the laundry, hoping he wouldn't know until too late. I checked through the window for any enchanted creatures then eased the door open.

Sunlight rained down on me as soon as I stepped outside the manor. I breathed in the air, tasting the freshness of it. With a smile, I ran away from the house.

I had almost made it to the trees when the female nymph came running toward me. She shook her head and pointed back to the manor.

"Not you, too," I said, slowing down.

She looked at me sadly with her wooden eyes.

"I wanted to check on you long ago, but he doesn't often let me out of his sight. Are you feeling better? I'm sorry for what happened."

She shrugged her shoulder and looked back into the trees. Her male counterpart waited there.

"Are you two together again?" I wasn't sure how else to word it.

She grinned widely, understanding, and nodded vigorously.

"I'm happy for that."

"Benella!" The vibrations of the beast's roar rumbled the ground, tickling the bottoms of my feet.

The nymphs shooed me toward the manor again.

With a sigh, I slowly turned around and walked back. He had sounded angry, but his mood didn't worry me. My slow pace was so I might enjoy more time outside.

He waited in the laundry room doorway. I clutched the sheet to me and stopped several paces away.

"What were you thinking, going outdoors without clothes?" he asked in a calm tone, but I could hear the frustration and anger underneath.

"I had the sheet."

He crooked a finger at me. I wrinkled my nose and didn't budge.

"I'm tired of being inside. I only wanted to walk around a bit. I was covered." I swept my hand down to indicate the sheet draped around me. "At least the important bits were covered."

He left the shelter of the doorway to stalk close to me. He circled me, inspecting the wrapping then stopped directly behind me. His breath tickled my hair a moment before his lips skimmed the exposed skin of my shoulder.

"All of your bits are important," he said, moving aside my hair to kiss the back of my neck before continuing on to the opposite shoulder. "I would like them all covered when you go out."

When he finished with the shoulder, he moved to the

side of my neck. With guilty pleasure, I tipped my head to the side to give him better access.

He growled and pulled me against his chest. His erection pressed against me.

"If you can stay inside and out of the study unless absolutely necessary, I will have the letters ready by morning," he said, planting a kiss along my jaw.

His fingers closed around my hand, and he led me back inside where steaming water filled the largest washtub.

"Please wait until I leave before getting into the water."

He pressed his lips to my shoulder once more then quickly left.

I tingled all over. Pent energies, indeed.

THOUGH I'D HOPED to go directly to the Water, the beast insisted I ride to Konrall first. I had two letters to deliver there. I couldn't find it in myself to be too upset by the stop, however. I wore clothes; a plain dress to look respectable and underthings. I grinned to myself.

Swiftly brought me to Konrall in record time and halted before the candle maker's door. He knelt so I could dismount with grace and watched as I knocked.

It took a moment, but eventually the door opened and a familiar smile greeted me.

"Good day, Benella. Regretfully, the merchant isn't due for a few more days."

I realized he thought I'd arrived looking for payment from the last flower delivery.

"I'm actually here to bring you a letter," I said, pulling out the beast's note. It had the candle maker's name on it and a wax seal. Nothing else.

"Oh, from your father?"

"I'm afraid I don't know. I'm sure reading it will enlighten you. I have another to deliver to the butcher for the Kinlyn family, so I'd best be on my way."

The candle maker nodded absently as he stared at the seal.

The butcher was just as curious about the letter for the Kinlyn's that I left in his care, but I didn't say anything more to him than I had to the candle maker.

When I exited the shop, Swiftly was not where I'd left him. Tennen had his mane and was watering him at the smithy. The baker stood beside Tennen.

"Convenient for a quiet conversation with you," the butcher said from just behind me.

I nodded and looked back at him with a smile.

"Yes, if I were dull enough to march over there to claim my horse."

"Do you want me to fetch him for you?" he asked.

"No need."

I called for Swiftly, keeping my voice calm and pleasant

so as not to upset the creature. However, it didn't seem to matter.

Swiftly pulled his head out of the water so abruptly that he yanked his mane out of Tennen's grasp. The horse then pivoted on his back legs and thundered toward me. In an instant, he stopped and dropped to his knees. The practicality of not using reins became very evident.

The butcher chuckled behind me.

"A well trained mount."

Already on Swiftly's back, I agreed.

"Keeps me out of trouble."

Swiftly stood as the baker called my name. I smiled my farewell to the butcher then leaned over Swiftly.

"I don't trust the pair of them. Best not to let them too close."

Swiftly bobbed his head and snorted in a very horse-like fashion. He closed the distance between the baker and me at a trot then came to a quivering stop, his ears laid back as he listened.

"Good day, Mr. Medunge," I said politely before glancing at Tennen, who still stood in the shadows of the smithy.

"Thank you for watering my horse," I called to him with a sweet smile. Tennen glared at me.

The baker took a step toward Swiftly, reclaiming my attention as the horse sidestepped.

"Has your father mentioned my visit?" the baker asked.

"I've been away and am just now going to see my father," I said.

"Away. Yes, your father mentioned you are an employed woman now. Such a shame for someone of your beauty to have to work so hard." He clucked his tongue. "I spoke to your father of several other options should you want a better life than a maid, but I'll let him discuss them with you."

I nodded farewell and tapped my heel to Swiftly. We quickly left Konrall.

The first letter I delivered in the Water was to the Head. Again, the man didn't receive me, but his assistant took the letter and assured me it would find its way into the Head's hands later in the day.

The last two letters I delivered in one stop. One was simply addressed to the Whispering Sisters and the other to my father. Ila greeted me as usual with tea at the door, but her smile was hesitant.

"You've been gone so long I thought perhaps Aryana truly upset you."

I hugged Ila close because I was so happy to see a friend.

"Not at all. Well, maybe at first, but my master's demand on my time is what kept me away so long."

"Everything is well, then?" she asked.

"Yes. I have a letter for you from my master and one for my father."

"I will take you to your father first."

We walked a familiar hall, and she stopped before his door. When she opened it, Father looked surprised, but happy, to see me there.

"Excuse me, please," he said, speaking comfortably now to the sisters he taught. He came to me and hugged me tightly.

"Had you not visited today," he said, pulling back, "I would have walked to you."

"I apologize for the delay." I reached into my bag and handed Father the letter the beast had penned. "He asked me to wait an extra day so he could send a letter with me."

Father glanced at the seal then tucked the letter in his jacket.

"I shall save this for later," he said, patting the pocket that hid it. "Have you spoken to Bryn?"

"I came straight here. I will visit with her before I go."

He nodded and promised to meet me at the house for the midday meal.

Ila led me to the bathing rooms where Aryana waited. Since I would join Father soon, I declined a bath and sat on the cushion beside her tub.

"What brings you today?" Aryana asked.

"I have a letter addressed to the Whispering Sisters."

I took the letter from my bag and held it out for either of them to take. Ila made no move toward it, and Aryana smiled at her before holding out her hand.

Unlike the rest, she barely glanced at the seal before breaking it and reading the contents. A moment later she laughed, low, rough, and amused. She handed the note to me, surprising me.

STOP EDUCATING HER. She is a smart, clever woman and should be left to discover the world and its pleasures first hand.

I FROWNED AT THE LETTER, then looked up to meet Ila's amused gaze as she too read the words.

"So you've spoken to your master about what you've learned here?" Aryana questioned lightly.

"I've kept my word," I said. "I've only mentioned that I visit my friends here. What I've learned has stayed with me."

She grinned.

"I think that's his issue. Has he tried to seduce you?"

I blushed.

"And thanks to our education, it didn't work?"

I shook my head because it hadn't been what the sisters had taught me that had kept me the most safe. I felt a slight sadness again for Bryn and Sara.

"It wasn't what I learned here as much what I've learned out there." They both made small noises of understanding. "I should go speak with Bryn," I said with a sigh and stood.

"No questions for us today?" Aryana asked.

"It might be better if I didn't. I wouldn't want to cause you trouble."

Aryana snorted.

"He doesn't worry me. I worry more about you under his roof. Take care. We are here if you need us."

I nodded and left.

Swiftly followed me to my old home and waited outside while I went in. Bryn sat at the table, speaking excitedly to a woman I didn't know. When Bryn saw me, some of the light left her eyes. The woman turned to me with an expectant smile.

"Dana," Bryn said, "this is my other sister, Benella."

"Another sister?" Dana said. "My, I didn't know there were so many of you. I don't think she was in the dinner count. I'd best go and add another place," she said, standing and leaning over to kiss Bryn's cheek.

"It's not necessary," Bryn said, standing as well. "Benella often doesn't have time for us."

Her words, though spoken politely, irritated me. She hadn't even consulted me to see if I might attend.

"Is this for your wedding dinner?" I asked.

"Of course," Dana said with a laugh. "Three nights from now, your sister will be married to my cousin. It will be a feast the Water will not soon forget."

How could Bryn think I would miss her wedding feast?

"Then I shall be there," I said, returning Dana's smile. She seemed truly excited by the dinner and the marriage.

"I'll leave you to visit," she said as she moved to the door.

After she left, Bryn turned on me. I didn't wait for whatever grief she intended to air.

"Are you well? How is the baby?" I asked.

She sighed, her expression between anger and excitement.

"The babe is fine, making my middle thicker. I told Edmund I suspected I might be carrying. He turned a bit green but assured me he is excited by the prospect." She eyed my dress. "Edmund's father is well connected with the most successful merchants in the Water. Dana assured me it will be a formal affair. Blye has been working nonstop on our dresses. She won't have time to make one for you, too. Not this late."

Was that her only concern? The way I would dress?

"I'm certain I will not embarrass you."

She looked at my dress in doubt, and I distracted her with another question.

"Were you able to fix Father's coat?"

Her face flushed, and she glanced down at the table. Guilt painted her face.

"Someone in town saw Father going to the Whispering Sisters and discovered he worked there. Can you believe he would purposely tarnish our reputations like that? We spoke about it, and he agreed it would be best if he did not attend the dinner or my wedding."

"You suggested he not attend?" I asked in disbelief.

"It would have been awkward. His association with *them...*" She shook her head.

I couldn't believe my ears. She didn't want her own father to attend because he taught whores, giving them an education they could use to change their profession. The only reason Father taught there was to provide for us, for her. And, what about the merchants attending her dinner who visited the Sisters for other reasons? They were still good enough for Bryn.

"Who is paying for this dinner?" I asked, feeling disgusted with her.

"Edmund's father knows our situation so he offered to pay a portion."

"And the rest?"

She didn't meet my eyes.

"Father assured me he had been saving for just such an event."

I thought of the two gold I'd given for the hair oil. No doubt the change had gone toward Bryn's feast, but that wouldn't have been enough. I swung my gaze to the almost barren bookshelves. My heart broke for my father.

"You could have helped," Bryn accused. "When you forage, you always find something worth trading. I asked you to come back with something to trade, and you always return with nothing. It's as if you think you no longer have a responsibility to your family."

No responsibility? I'd sacrificed myself to save Father's life and set them all free.

"Tell Father I couldn't stay, but that I will visit again soon," I spoke through clenched teeth as I moved to the door.

"I understand if you don't want to attend," she called as I left.

So I was an embarrassment to her, too? I wanted to scream and hit something.

Swiftly sensed my mood and laid his ears back as I mounted.

"Home, Swiftly," I said harshly.

CHAPTER TEN

STILL SEETHING, I CRASHED THROUGH THE KITCHEN DOOR and searched for something to throw. Bryn had gone too far. How could she so publicly disassociate herself from our father? The man who'd given everything to care for us. He never asked for anything in return. He'd known about Bryn's interest in Tennen, her money hoarding, and he accepted it. Accepted *her*.

Stalking into the room, I found a platter of fruit on the table. I hefted the tray, ready to throw it into the fireplace when it was plucked from my hands.

"And what, dearest, has you so agitated? Surely the letters didn't cause this," the beast said quietly beside me.

I spun to face him.

"My sister told my father that she doesn't want him at her wedding feast. Can you believe her? After all he's given. He's good enough to pay for her wedding feast but not to attend." I tossed my hands high into the air in my frustration then sat heavily on a chair. "I think she meant to exclude me, too, had it not been for her betrothed's cousin. Bryn hinted that the way I dress would embarrass her."

He set the platter to the side and studied me intently for a moment.

"What do you plan to do?" he finally asked.

"What do you mean?"

"Revenge. Will you tell Edmund about the baby?"

"Of course not. It would only cause more pain to the people I care about." I paused and frowned at the beast. "How do you know his name?"

He gave a small smile. "I like to be kept current on what your family is doing. I wouldn't want any surprises to take you from me."

His comment struck a chord in me. And, I realized I wouldn't want to be taken from him either. Especially if it meant living with Bryn again.

"I wish my sister would see what she's doing," I said with a sigh.

"Perhaps you should tell her what a selfish bitch she is."

I gave him a sharp look. I might have been mad at her, but I still loved her and didn't like anyone speaking ill of her.

He gave a deprecating laugh and shook his head.

"It's the truth. I well know selfish."

176

"She won't listen."

"You are very persuasive," he said.

I sighed again.

"The feast is in three days. I do want to attend, and I want to bring my father. I will need Swiftly again. Do you have a coat that might fit my father? I would return it."

The beast nodded slowly.

"I can provide what's needed for both you and your father. But I need your word that you will return before sunset."

"Of course," I agreed easily, glad that he didn't mention it would be an extra visit.

As a precaution, I went to bed fully dressed. Having clothes again was nice, and I hoped to keep them. However, when I woke I was once again naked. The beast lay curled next to me, sleeping peacefully.

Warm and comfortable, I stayed in bed a moment. His dreams never seemed troubled when he slept beside me, and I was glad my presence gave him some measure of comfort; he seemed to derive very little elsewhere.

I studied his sleep-relaxed face. Where others might see a wild brute, I saw a bored, clever creature who had forgotten what it meant to be a man—if he ever really knew. I wasn't blind to his faults, just as I wasn't blind to his regrets.

Quietly, I slid from the bed and moved to the wash water as I continued to consider the beast.

His past misconducts had brought him fifty years of questionable punishment. A punishment that didn't inspire reform but, rather, loneliness.

I ran the cloth over my face and wondered if that wasn't the real reason he'd brought me here. Yes, he wanted to break the curse; but, perhaps, he had wanted a companion more. I rinsed the cloth and wiped my arms and torso.

The drag of cloth over my breast distracted me from my thoughts and brought forward the memory of his mouth on me. My nipples tightened. Since he'd first set his mouth on them, they felt more...alive. Perhaps I was only more aware.

I rinsed the cloth again, and a furry chest pressed against my back as if my thoughts had conjured him. I froze. His fingers trailed down my arm, leaving goosebumps in their wake.

"Beauty," he whispered.

His lips pressed against the curve of my shoulder as he stole the cloth from my grasp and set it against my stomach. I couldn't move. The cloth skimmed over my skin, from ribs to navel, while his breath tickled my neck.

"Allow me to help," he said.

The cloth sank lower until it swept over my curls. My breath hitched. He stopped and swept up over my stomach again and further still, until it smoothed over my breast. I leaned back against him and forgot to breathe as he gently circled one then the other.

When the cloth left my chest and drifted lower, I reached back and set my hand to his cheek. He turned his head and kissed my palm. All the while, the cloth continued its downward glide. My skin heated, and a burning ignited in my middle when the cloth swiped over my curls once more. Without meaning to, I widened my stance and then almost groaned when he retreated without exploring further.

"Please," I whispered, trembling.

He growled low and worked his way down again. This time, he parted me and gently ran the cloth over me. Once. I gasped. Twice. I panted. Thrice. My legs shook. He removed the cloth and set it on the wash bowl.

My insides had liquefied. I *wanted*, but I didn't understand what. I *ached,* but couldn't name an exact spot.

His fingers trailed over the skin of my arms and stomach. He swept my hair aside and pressed his lips against my neck, nuzzling and licking. The attention caused tingles and shocks to course through me, ending between my legs.

He prowled around me, his arm supporting my back. His hungry gaze held mine for a moment, then he dipped his head and suckled my nipple, causing a sweet ache that made me groan. He growled in response and nudged me back a step...two. I bumped against the bed.

He lowered me to the mattress, grasped my hands, and

held them slightly out to my sides. His mouth roamed my chest, then lower. Too consumed by heat, I didn't protest.

His tongue touched my curls, and I gave a soft whimper. My hips lifted of their own accord. He teased me, never going lower to the spot that ached so badly for his touch. My muscles tensed from anticipation. I whined and shifted when he skimmed by me again. Heat crested and ebbed, rolling over me in confusing waves. Gasping, I struggled for air as the tension coiled tighter.

Then his lips, his touch, left me. Cool air confused me. I lifted my head. The room was empty. Letting my head fall, I stared at the ceiling as I realized how close I'd come to letting him taste me. Oddly, the thought didn't disturb me.

Slowly, my breathing and pulse returned to normal. Though I physically recovered, mentally I replayed the encounter until I frowned with annoyance and understanding. Pent energies. He'd woken something inside me with patience and persistence. Whatever it was, I wanted something only he understood. Well, others might understand; however, he was the only one likely to tell me about it.

I stood and moved to the wardrobe, surprised to see he'd given me a full selection once again. Though I eyed the plain dresses and even the shirts and pants, I did not move to wear them. The remembered feel of his lips stopped me.

Moving around dresses, I found one of the gossamer

types he'd first made me wear and grinned. Taking the dress and a shirt, I prepared myself for an interesting day.

Awhile later, I stepped through the study door, carrying a tray.

When he glanced at me, he froze. The shirt reached the top of my thighs just barely covering the v of my legs. I'd buttoned the hole just above my breasts and left the rest loose, exposing flesh from the valley between my breasts and everything downward each time I moved. Yet, the gossamer dress underneath the shirt gave the illusion of decency.

"Did you eat?" I asked politely, setting the tray on his desk.

He shook his head slightly, not taking his gaze from my body. I felt like stretching, to bask in his attention, which I thought odd since I'd always had it.

"What are you wearing?" he finally managed.

"A compromise, I hope," I said with a smile. "You want to see me. I want to feel covered. This is a little bit of both, don't you agree?"

I held out my arms, which inadvertently lifted the hem of my shirt by two inches and parted the edges. I executed a slow turn for him. Before I knew what had happened, he had me up in his arms, and we raced through the halls back to my room.

"It is better to wear nothing," he growled, setting me on my bed and stripping me of the clothes. The fabric tore in his haste. He sank to his knees and looked up at me.

"I'm begging you, stay in your room today. You will want for nothing."

I nodded, disappointed. I'd hoped for more from him.

His hungry gaze swept over my face, then he closed his eyes. In that moment, I understood that he'd wanted more from me, too.

Blushing deeply, I inched my knees apart.

With his eyes still closed, he gave a groan and kissed my knee.

I inched my knees further apart. He opened his eyes. His gaze locked with mine. Then, he leaned forward and kissed the side of my knee. Further still saw a kiss a few inches up. Barely breathing, I leaned back on my elbows and boldly drew up my legs and placed my heels on the edge of the bed, giving him the view he'd wanted just a few days ago.

My cheeks burned with uncertainty and wanting.

"I will not take," he said. "Tell me what you want from me."

"Taste me. No more," I begged.

He obliged, leaning forward to run his tongue along the crease of my hip and thigh. I fought not to squirm.

I felt myself part and his breath on my center. His tongue touched inside, just skimming to the left of my opening, missing the spot that burned for his attention. He shifted his focus to the right side, giving it the same. My hands drifted to his head. Then, his tongue touched my center. My hips bucked as he skimmed it lightly, at first, then with more urgency. When his lips closed over it and he suckled, noises escaped me. Moans and whimpers.

Gasping, I arched my hips. He closed his hands around my thighs. The firm touch of his fingers aroused me further. He left my center to tease my opening, dipping in for a small taste before plunging the length of his tongue into me. He lapped and sucked for a moment, all the while the area he'd left cried for more attention.

He seemed to sense my need because he returned to it and suckled with greater intensity. The tension inside me coiled tighter and tighter. By reflex, my legs tried to stiffen and close. His firm grip kept them open, enabling his feast until the coiled tension inside me broke free with a scream. I convulsed, thrusting up into his flicking tongue as my legs locked in their stretched position. Waves of pleasure coursed through me, tightening and releasing my muscles in slow rolling waves.

His licking eased as I twitched under him. I lay limp on the bed, a new world suddenly exposed to me. He kissed my sensitive nub lightly then the inside of my thigh. While I was still too weak to speak, he rose and left me there in a puddle of awe.

After several long minutes, I regained enough control to stand up and wash myself again. Every nerve ending still tingled. I felt relaxed and at ease. Sara's cry of delight and look of shame afterward made sense. To feel that way with the baker between her legs had to be deeply disturbing. But the beast. I sighed in contentment before I caught myself.

Sitting heavily, I gave my circumstances careful deliberation. If the beast freed himself, he would undoubtedly forget me. That he would probably disregard me easily made me uncomfortably morose. I certainly wouldn't forget him. Yet, once he was free, I would need to move on with my life. After Bryn wed, I would need to start my own search for a suitable man. However, the thought of marrying some unknown man caused my heart to lurch, and I realized just how much I'd grown to care for the beast. What I'd told him about leaving me a piece of myself was more true now, than ever.

I wouldn't be the same if he took everything I had. I wouldn't be able to walk away.

But, if he did not free himself, would saving a piece of myself be an issue? If he remained a beast, I could stay with him as long as I wanted.

Frowning, I considered his attitude toward Rose and amended my thought. I could stay with him as long as I had my youth. After that, I could still find someone suitable to wed. But, the prospect of doing so didn't fill me with any sense of anticipation.

Pushing aside the dread, I focused on the immediate possibilities and made a decision. I would stay here with the beast; not because of a threat I no longer believed him capable of carrying out, but because I wanted to stay.

Not bothering to dress, I stood with a smile and went to seek him out. To my dismay, both doors were locked.

A horrible thought struck, and I flew to my window. Thrusting open the glass, I leaned out and called for Egrit. She came into view after several moments. Relief flooded me.

She looked up at me and shrugged as if asking why I called.

"I'm so sorry to yell like that. I was worried. The beast has locked me in my room, and I wanted to be sure you were safe."

The nymph smiled and nodded. She waved me back inside, and I quickly obeyed, realizing I hung out the window with my breasts completely exposed.

Blushing, I sat on the bed.

"Sir?" I called after a few moments. "It's cruel to lock me in my room without telling me what I did wrong. I thought...what we did..." I sighed, suddenly uncomfortable with the thought that I may have asked him to do something he hadn't wanted to do.

"I apologize if I insisted on something that wasn't appropriate."

A mist filtered into the room, blocking out all light.

"Is this really necessary? We are capable of talking, aren't we?"

Just as quickly as the mists came, they left. Next to me on the bed, lay a tray stocked with food, drink, books, and a letter.

. . .

Dearest,

You did nothing wrong nor is there any need to apologize. I'm asking you to stay in your room for your safety while I work in the study on estate business. If you have further suggestions for distraction, please speak them aloud. I will need them.

Please refrain from hanging out windows unclothed. It upsets me.

Forever your servant.

I FINISHED READING with a small smile.

"The ledgers and records are a fount of knowledge as are the books in the library. These lands used to be productive beyond the growth and sales of flowers. I think that is why there are so many books on farming and such."

Picking up a book, I reclined on the bed and settled in to read.

HE LEFT me in my room for three days. The relaxed ease I felt after he had tasted me quickly disappeared until I paced my room in agitation.

"This afternoon is my sister's wedding feast," I called, looking out the window at the colorful dawn. I felt like throwing something again. Instead, I marched over to his door and kicked it.

"You said I could go. You promised to provide me with everything I needed."

When I turned around, the large tub from the laundry sat near the end of my bed. Curls of steam drifted up from the water. Marching over to it, I slid in with a hiss and quickly washed, using the hair oil from Ila.

A towel rested on the edge of the tub when I opened my eyes. Rising from the water, pink from the heat, I toweled my skin. My mood improved only slightly with the bath.

I walked to the wardrobe and opened it. Inside waited a single dress, exquisite in its simplicity. On the floor was a pair of matching slippers. No underclothes were present.

I lifted the gown over my head and let the delicate material drift down my arms and body. It fit perfectly, but I frowned at the scooped neckline and the puckered outline of my nipples through the fabric. Though the material was not see-through, it was so fine it hardly seemed appropriate. Yet, he had given me no other options.

The door to my room unlatched and creaked open. I quickly stepped into the slippers and drifted to the door.

The hallway stood empty. Disappointed, I made my way to the kitchen and opened the outer door. Just outside, Swiftly waited. Again, there was no sign of the beast. It was so unlike him to allow me to leave without saying farewell and asking for assurance that I would return. Yet, given our last encounter, I understood his reason for staying away and applauded his progress in self-denial and control.

Swiftly quickly knelt, his ears flicking forward and back in apparent agitation. I smoothed a hand along his neck and mounted, wondering at his mood. However, his huff as my bare bottom settled on his back with only the skirt separating us wasn't a mystery.

"Sorry," I whispered. The creature shook his head and set off.

I rode straight to the Sisters. I needed help with my hair and assurances about the dress. Even though they didn't wear clothes, I trusted they knew what was fashionable.

Ila met me at the door with a wide smile.

"You look stunning. For your sister's feast?"

I nodded as I drank down the tea.

"Come to my room, I will do your hair."

Sitting on Ila's dressing stool, I relaxed as she wove my hair into several beautiful, twisting braids.

"Everyone there will forget your sister is the focus of the evening," Ila said, tucking the last braid. I smiled at her compliment and hoped Bryn would have no issue with my appearance...or Father's.

"Is Father here?"

"He asked not to work today. You will find him at home."

Standing, I hugged her and thanked her for her help. Before I left, I looked back over my shoulder.

"Is it too daring?" I asked, letting the uncertainty I felt show. "The dress?"

"The dress is beautiful, as are you," she assured me.

I glanced down at my breasts. Though the material was not transparent, I could still see details, not in color, but in shape.

"I don't want to shame my father," I said softly.

She smiled sadly and walked me to the door. Just behind it rested a fine black cloak that complemented the silver of the dress. "Here. Take this for today, until you feel comfortable. You will see that your dress is not so unusual."

I thanked her with yet another hug and placed the cloak around my shoulders before walking to my father's home. He answered the door with a happy smile. Thankfully, Bryn and Blye were both absent.

"I've been waiting for you." He pulled me into a tight hug. "I've missed you."

"I'm sorry I left before we could speak," I said, referring to my last visit. He waved off my apology and motioned for me to sit. I kept my cloak on, but he didn't comment.

"How have things been for you?" I asked, noting his healthy weight and complexion.

"I enjoy teaching the sisters," he said openly. "They are kind and gentle."

"And Bryn and Blye?"

He sighed.

"They are well but have learned where I teach. Blye has

moved into a small room above the seamstress's shop, and Bryn is staying with Dana, Edmund's cousin, until the wedding."

"What a relief," I said with an impish smile. "Finally, you can eat your own food and relax in your own home."

He nodded, but a sad smile crossed his face.

"If only he would release you to come back home."

His comment caused an odd pang because, even for my father, I didn't want to leave the beast. Over the course of our weeks together, he'd won my affection; and through his progress to becoming a better man, he'd won my respect.

"The baker mentioned his visit," I said, changing the subject and pushing thoughts of the beast from my mind. "He said he spoke to you about several options if I didn't want to be a maid anymore."

"He offered for your hand."

I made a face, and he nodded.

"I know your feelings about the man and told him I could not accept his offer. He insisted I speak with you of his wealth and the position he would guarantee you."

The image of Sara on the dough table rose in my mind, and I knew with certainty that he offered a position I would not like.

"His wealth makes no difference in my aversion of the man," I said.

Father agreed, and we chatted for several hours before he asked if I was happy.

"I am, and will be even more so if you accompany me to the feast."

"I don't think I have a choice." He stood and fetched a box and letter. He handed me the letter.

GUARD *your daughter carefully in my absence. She must return to me before sunset.*

IT BORE the same seal the beast had used before. I looked up as Father opened the box. Inside rested a dignified suit coat, crisp shirt and neck cloth, and new pants to match. I smiled at the beast's thoughtfulness.

"When did this arrive?" I asked.

"Three days ago."

I insisted Father go dress. While I waited, a rapid tap sounded at the door. Opening it, I was surprised to see Mr. Crow hopping around on the ground outside. A small white piece of parchment was tied to his leg. I bent to remove it, ignoring his squawking.

The heavy scrawl on the paper was almost illegible with ink spills and rips where the beast had written too forcefully.

RETURN AT ONCE.

· · ·

I TURNED THE PAPER OVER, but the other side remained blank.

"I don't understand," I whispered to Mr. Crow.

He tilted his head at me and hopped forward. His beak gently worried my dress.

"He agreed I could go. He sent my father clothes. He can't ask me to return before the ceremony. Assure him I will return before sunset. I will keep my word."

The crow cawed loudly then took flight.

Closing the door, I waited for my father to emerge.

"You look so dapper," I said when he did.

He grinned at me and gave a little bow. No one would find fault in his appearance; the jacket was fashionable and fit him well.

"Let's dine together," he said, offering his arm.

We strolled down the market street to a small pub that served respectable families. Father offered to take my cloak as he held out a chair for me. Not wanting to draw attention, I surrendered it and quickly sat. When he took the chair across from me, his eyes swept my dress.

"I understand his warning now," he said.

I blushed and remained quiet. Though worry shone lightly in his expression, I saw no real rebuke. Cautiously, I glanced at the other women in the room. None wore a dress woven as fine as mine, and I caught their envious stares. No one's regard held any censure.

After our meal, we made our way to the Head's home. In the backyard, many had gathered to see Bryn wed

Edmund. Near the back of the gathering, Father helped me from my cloak and caught my nervous look.

"Head high, Bini. You are lovely."

With his approval, I walked by his side to our seats near the pretty flower arch where Bryn would say her vows. Murmurs quieted as we passed. I kept a polite smile on my mouth and held my father's arm tightly.

Once we sat, we only had to wait a few moments before a sweet soprano rang out in a merry song about joining and love. When it quieted, the crowd turned to see Bryn and her fiancé walking down the aisle toward the arch. The Head followed them.

The simple ceremony didn't last long, but the well wishes and speeches took until the evening meal. I held myself still through it all, even though I wanted to fidget and shift on my seat to bring the blood and life back into my buttocks.

Bryn glowed with happiness as she clung to Edmund's arm. He looked equally pleased.

Father and I rose and followed the new couple from the Head's yard to the public room where Dana hosted the feast. I stopped to hug Bryn, bringing her attention to Father and me for the first time. Her smile hardened at the sight of us, but she did not turn away.

"I'm so happy you came. You look lovely," she said to me.

Then, she looked at Father and complimented him on

his handsome garb. I could see the calculation in her eyes and suppressed a sigh.

Father and I sat and watched many others pour through the doors. Bryn hadn't lied about the merchants who would attend. Many saw me sitting close to the bride and groom and asked for an introduction. Their unwelcome attention just served to irritate my sister further.

Finally, everyone sat and the meal began. Course after course slowly emerged from the kitchen. There was a time when I would have appreciated spending hours eating the wonderful dishes set before me. However, I couldn't find any joy in this meal. Instead, I watched the shadows shift in the room as the afternoon progressed.

With relief, I leaned toward Father when it was time for me to go. He guessed my purpose before I spoke.

"It is time for us to take our leave," he said softly to my sister.

She paused in her conversation with a merchant who had stopped to talk and nodded her farewell. It was brief and uncaring.

I turned to Blye and gave her a hug, whispering good-bye. At least Blye didn't seem resentful of my presence, though she didn't speak to Father at all.

On our way to the door, several men of influence stopped Father. He politely ended the conversation as soon as he could, but the sun never paused its sinking progress.

When we finally reached the door, the golden orb hovered dangerously close to the horizon.

"I must hurry," I said, giving Father a hug outside.

"I didn't realize how late it was. Will you be all right?" Father pulled back to look at me with concern.

"I'll be fine." I kissed his cheek and gave him the cloak.

"Return this to Ila, please. Thank her for me." I turned away from him and called for Swiftly.

His hooves thundered nearby, then he was kneeling before me. I quickly climbed up and clasped his mane.

"Good night, Father," I said as Swiftly stood. "I'll see you soon."

I leaned low over Swiftly as he turned and galloped through the streets.

"Before the sun sets," I said, encouraging him to lengthen his stride.

The wind cooled my skin under my gown and tugged at my hair. I kept an eye on the sun the length of the journey. We made it through the gates just as the last light faded.

The sight of the waiting, roiling cloud of mist brought fierce joy to me. I'd missed him and hadn't known it until just then.

I slid from Swiftly and sent him away with a pat on the neck. He shied around the mist while I walked straight toward it.

"I'm going to fall and hurt myself," I said.

Suddenly, I was up in the beast's arms, cradled against his chest. I sighed and leaned my head against him, content to close my eyes and run my fingers through his fur. I was home.

He brought me into the kitchen and set me on my feet. The continued silence and mist worried me.

"No mist," I said, stepping forward to touch him. The mist disappeared instantly. His angry eyes swept me from head to toe.

"You look tumbled," he said, his growl garbling his words.

"Windblown from the race home."

"Home," he sighed and closed his eyes.

"Why are you so upset?"

He opened his eyes, his gaze sweeping over me.

"That is not the dress I gave you."

"Of course it is. It was in the wardrobe."

He exhaled slowly.

"Rose replaced the dress I had with this." He gestured at my dress. "When I discovered the change...what man who saw you in this would let you go?"

The insecurity behind his words made me ache for him, and I realized something vital that I'd overlooked. I'd protected my body from him but not my heart. And while I wasn't watching, he'd touched it, leaving me marked by his gentle caring. I could no longer imagine my life without the beast.

I stepped close and rested my hand on his chest.

"No man can capture me, only a beast."

He lifted my hand to his mouth and kissed the palm while his heated gaze searched my face. Was he so unsure of my loyalty?

With a hammering heart, I shrugged one shoulder, easing the sleeve down to expose the top of my breast. His gaze drifted down and stayed riveted on my skin. My nipples reacted, and I knew that he saw. He lifted a finger and traced the outline.

I closed my eyes and pressed my hand over his, holding him to my breast.

"No man," I said again. "Only a beast."

A pained sound escaped him, and he picked me up again and brought me to my room, gently laying me on my bed.

This time wasn't slow and teasing. He tore the dress from me and latched onto the peak of my right breast, suckling roughly. Each pull sent a sizzle of desire straight between my legs. He shifted his attention to the other breast. I sighed with pleasure and threaded my fingers in his fur. His mouth nibbled a quick trail down, and his fingers dug into my thighs as he spread me wide. His breath tickled me for a heartbeat then his tongue laved me from opening to curls. Again and again, a long, slow stroke that had my hips twitching. When he closed his lips over my nub and suckled, I moaned.

"Yes," I whispered, liking the feeling.

My tension coiled higher as he tongued my opening, licking and sucking as I thrust my hips to meet his plunge.

I felt wild, uncontrolled. My legs stiffened, but his hands kept me wide. His mouth found my nub again to suck and flick. A cry burst from me as the tension broke in a torrent of fried nerve endings. I convulsed under his mouth, enjoying each pulse.

Finally, the sensation faded, and my hands fell to the mattress. What felt like hours of pleasure, took only minutes.

As before, he left me. This time, I fell asleep, legs spread wide and still dangling off the mattress.

I WOKE SNUGGLED AGAINST HIM. He kissed me softly but didn't touch me any further.

"Good morning," I whispered shyly. He'd tasted me twice, but this was the first time I'd actually faced him afterward.

"Good morning," he rumbled, combing his fingers through my unfettered hair.

I frowned at the feeling.

"Did you remove the braids?"

"I did...after I returned."

I blinked, understanding his meaning. "I'm sorry it didn't work."

He grunted then surprised me.

"It didn't work because I don't want it to work. I refuse to play her game any longer. I am content to stay as I am...if you will stay with me. Marry me," he said quietly.

My heart expanded at his unexpected proposal, and I knew I wanted nothing more than to say yes. Yet, I knew I could not. His revulsion of Rose held my tongue. Enchanted, he would never age; and one day, he would hold me in as much contempt as he did Rose. My heart broke at the thought, and I struggled to find the right answer to appease him.

I sat up, and he moved off the bed to watch me.

"I will leave something for your husband. I will leave you a virgin." He bent to a knee and placed a kiss on my bare stomach. "Will you marry me?" he repeated.

My heart jumped and fluttered in excitement despite my best efforts to quell it. If I married him, he would *be* my husband.

"Well, that's a convenient way to get around it, isn't it?"

He grinned, but it didn't reach his eyes. "I thought so." He remained on his knee. "And your answer?"

"I can't marry you," I said softly. After a hard swallow, I gave him the only reason I could speak aloud. "When I think of you, I have only these titles in my head: sir, master, liege lord, and beast. Where in there is your real name? I know too little about you."

He stood and nodded, surprisingly calm with my answer. Holding out a hand, he helped me to my feet. His gaze swept over me, bringing a light blush to my cheeks.

"Let's spend today together," he said.

"I need a moment first."

He nodded and left the room.

As soon as the door closed, I collapsed back onto the bed. What had I done? Somehow, along the way, I'd given the beast my heart. He would surely crush it within his too powerful grasp before he even realized he held it. Yet, I couldn't regret his keeping of my love. Because now, an imagined world without the beast seemed a horrible, lonely place. I was where I belonged.

After I relieved myself and washed, I went to the wardrobe. It was completely empty again. I smiled and moved to the door.

He waited for me in the hallway, as usual, and held out a hand. I wrapped my fingers in his and followed him to the library. A tray waited for us. He motioned for me to sit on the couch and proceeded to feed me bits of fruit.

"My name is Alec. When I was four, my father gave me my first horse, a pony really. I can barely remember what it looked like but remember thinking it enormous, until Father and I went on our first ride together." He chuckled at the memory. "I wish I could remember more of my life before he passed away."

"What about your youth with your mother?"

"After my father died, a large responsibility fell to her. She didn't have the advantage of a teacher for a father and struggled to learn so much in those first years. I didn't understand it then, but I see it now. Back then, I only knew that she was very busy."

"What did you do when she wasn't busy?" I asked, not liking the sad look he had.

We spent the rest of the day talking about our childhoods.

ON THE FOURTH morning since my return from the wedding, I ate in my room. The tray had been waiting for me beside my bed, and I knew he had slept with me at least a portion of the night. However, like the morning before, I woke alone.

Though we spent a good portion of our days together, and I remained naked, he had yet to touch me again. Instead, he spent his time telling me of his past, good and bad. I felt compassion for the lonely little boy he'd been but had a hard time understanding the selfish man he'd become. Though his mother had been busy, she'd loved him deeply.

I understood that he told me stories of his past so I could better know him, yet it didn't achieve his purpose. Those stories told me who he had been and gave some insight into how he'd become enchanted. Yet, they didn't tell me a thing about who he was now and what his hopes for the future might be. There were still so many questions I wanted to ask him. What did he like eating? What had he done to entertain himself since becoming enchanted? What had he thought the first time the villagers stormed the estate?

When I finished the food, I washed and left the room. Though we spent much time together, he excused himself often to work in his study. I didn't bring up the subject of my missing clothes, which I knew was the source of his need for distraction. I didn't want to diminish what he was achieving. Control over himself, regardless of the circumstance.

As I expected, I found him in his study, head bent over the estate records. He read them often, now. He even had pages of notes. Presently, he scratched something on a piece of parchment, lost to his thoughts.

"Good morning," I said from the door.

"Good morning." He lifted his gaze from his ledger to greet me but quickly returned to his reading.

"I was wondering...why did you spare me?"

"What do you mean?" he asked, maintaining his focus on the book before him.

"In the beginning, the first time you threw me over, I wasn't surprised by the net that caught me. The second time, I thought perhaps I'd just gotten lucky. But after...what was your reason?"

He looked up again and studied me with a peculiar expression.

"You didn't beg or stammer excuses. You accepted your fate but not with defeat."

Such a simple thing had saved me?

"Why did you offer me any one thing from the estate?"

A tension crept into his shoulders, and he looked down at his ledger again.

"Why are you asking so many questions?"

"I'm trying to know you better."

He sighed, and I knew he would answer.

"I wanted to give you a reason to return."

"And I did," I said with a smile.

"You did," he agreed solemnly. "The night you asked for refuge, I watched you try to start the fire. You worked calmly, despite the shivers shaking your hands. You didn't ask for help or balk at the task like other women I'd known. It upset me."

His admission surprised me.

"You wanted me to balk and ask for help?" I asked.

"No, after watching you, I wanted to keep you. But you'd only asked for refuge. So, I left you to see if your father had returned."

"Why did you want to keep me?"

"You ask too many questions," he said without rancor.

"Is that why you sent the trunk? To lure me back?" I smiled at him, though he wasn't looking at me. "Blye was quite interested in the cloth. I wonder how you would have fared with her."

He grunted, and I knew I'd amused him.

I left him to his work, knowing that I'd bothered him enough. I studied the bookshelves. Unsure what I wanted to read, I wandered for a bit. A lower shelf near the door caught my attention, and I bent to study the titles.

Something thumped to the floor in the study. I straightened and looked over my shoulder. The beast leaned over his desk, completely focused on me. On the floor before the desk was the estate book he'd just had open.

"Benella, dearest, please pick a book from the other side of the room," he said slowly.

I frowned for a moment. Why would he want me to...I recalled Ila bending in front of me to pet the cat. Before the threatening grin could burst forth, I nodded and moved out of his line of sight. Then, I grinned foolishly.

A WEEK LATER, I was feeling decidedly ignored and very unsure of myself. He'd stopped coming to my room at night and disappeared constantly; now, going so far as closing himself in the study.

I paced the library, trying to understand the turn in his behavior. It had started before Bryn's wedding. The first time he'd...I blushed and stopped my pacing to stare at the barred study. I'd thought his avoidance then might have meant we'd done something wrong, but he'd said we hadn't. Yet, his current actions seemed to suggest otherwise. Why else completely avoid me if not out of guilt?

Frustrated, I went and knocked on his door.

"Sir?" I still couldn't bring myself to use his given name.

"Yes," came his muffled answer. "Enter."

I walked in. As usual, he didn't look up. I nervously sat in a chair.

"I don't understand," I said.

That caught his attention. With a hint of worry, he looked up.

"What, dearest?"

"You said I didn't need to apologize, and you seemed to like tasting me. But you've stopped touching me completely. You don't look at me. You barely speak to me. I don't understand why."

He focused on his papers.

"Benella, now is not the best time for me to talk about—"

"Was it wrong? Are you ashamed of what we did? Should I be ashamed?" I couldn't get the image of Sara's shame from my head.

He stood abruptly and walked around the desk.

"No, Benella," he said, kneeling before me. "What we did should not cause you shame. I'm trying very hard to distract myself from thinking of those moments with you because I want to do it all again. But, I don't think I can taste you again and stop." He touched my face gently. "I want all of you. Please say you've reconsidered and will marry me."

I looked down at my hands, reflecting on what he'd just said. My fear remained. He would want me today or even ten years from now but certainly not beyond that. So I gave him the same answer as before.

"I know quite a bit about the old you, but still very little about who you are now. I know nothing about your hopes for the future beyond your desire to be free of the curse."

"The answer is still no, then."

Miserably, I nodded.

"May I please have clothes?"

He remained silent until I met his gaze.

"They are in your room."

CHAPTER ELEVEN

ONCE I WORE PROPER CLOTHES, HE SPENT MORE TIME WITH me. We talked for hours of inconsequential things and idled away our time with whatever struck our fancy. He no longer used his mist, and his growl was completely absent. I cherished each day spent with him but found time passed too quickly in his entertaining and courteous company. When each evening arrived, it always felt as if the sun had just risen.

At his insistence, I began to sleep in a plain white gown that stayed on me all night. He still came to my bed and held me while he rested, but only joined me once I already slept. When I woke, he was already gone, waiting for me in the hallway, ready to start a new, companionable day.

Through our time together, he began to share his hopes for his future as a beast; and he stopped trying to see Rose. However, he didn't ask me to marry him again. I thought he had perhaps come to the same conclusion I had. He would care for me easily in my youth, but not as I weathered.

I tried not to dwell on our future, and gave up trying to quell what I felt for him. I loved the beast and would never stop. I would stay with him for as long as he would have me.

Near the end of summer, an evening storm swept through the area, and the beast and I decided to linger by the fire in the library, one of our favorite pastimes. A warm fire lent a soft glow to the pre-twilight gloom as I reclined on the lounge. My bare feet were propped comfortably on the cushions, and the beast sat on the floor so he could idly run his fingers through my hair as I read aloud.

He stopped me occasionally to feed me some tidbit from the tray on the table or to ask a question about the text. I enjoyed both kinds of interruption.

When I finished the passage, I closed the book softly and sighed. Neither of us talked for a moment, both content as we were.

"I cannot recall when I have ever spent as pleasurable an evening as tonight," I said, twisting to look up at him.

He gave me a soft look and nodded. But I barely noticed. My words struck a deep chord, and the solution to his enchantment opened wide in my mind. I bolted upright with a jolt.

"Of course!"

He eyed me in concern.

"Did I witness an epiphany?"

I stared at him, torn. If I shared with him what I'd just realized, he could free himself and become a man and age like any other. Time would not make me leave. Yet, he wasn't any man. He was a lord. And what lord wanted a scholar's daughter, even in her youth? None. He would likely marry one of his own station. However, if I kept the information to myself, I would win a few more years of his consideration as a beast.

His caring gaze held mine, and I knew I couldn't keep the truth of my revelation from him. He'd suffered his punishment long enough.

I forced a wide grin and ignored the tightening in my chest.

"Yes, you did. A life changing one. If I asked you in what ways you might pleasure me, what would you say?"

"I would rather show you," he said with a playful growl and a leer.

"If I asked you what things please me, what would you say?"

"We are not talking about sexual pleasure any longer, are we?" he said. With a tender look, he studied me for a moment. "Books please you. Learning. Walking outside. Visiting with your father."

"So, if I were to ask you for a night of pleasure what would you do?"

His eyes widened, and I knew he'd come to the same

conclusion. For the past fifty years, he'd been trying to sexually please the enchantress for nothing.

A storm grew behind his eyes, and I quickly scrambled to my knees and gently held his face.

"You've spent time with her over the years. You must know something of what she likes," I whispered. "Go to her. Try something new."

He hesitated, and I saw it was because of me. It gave me a small hope. Perhaps a lord could care for a scholar's daughter. I gently ran my hand along the fur of his neck.

"I am content to stay here with you just as you are, but you are not the same beast you were. Your people need you. You need to bring prosperity back to the north."

He rose reluctantly, kissed my brow, and left the room.

Feeling bereft, I went to my room and tugged on a nightgown. My heart ached with what the new day might offer. There was the possibility for great happiness and even greater despair. I hoped that once he turned into a man, he would not forget me, as I'd long ago predicted.

I'd thought saving my virginity would be all I needed for a future husband because I'd never considered the possibility that the beast would claim my heart. I knew my foolishness now. If he cast me aside, the beast would hurt me as he'd promised he never would.

Sighing, I tried to let my worries and heartaches free; and gradually, sleep claimed me.

BEFORE THE SUN YET ROSE, a distant clatter of breaking dishes woke me, and I realized our attempt had failed. As much as I wanted to keep the beast, I wanted to set him free to be the man he should be.

I rose from bed and followed the sounds that continued as I hurried through the halls. A rather loud bang came from the direction of the kitchen, and my heart broke for the beast. I rushed to the room, then froze.

Tennen stood with a sack in one hand, stuffing it with enchanted food. He spotted me and froze in shock as well.

I recovered first, pivoted, and took off running. His steps rang out behind me. Too close. He caught me by my braid. I cried out as he tugged me back against his chest. My heart hammered. I bent forward slightly, intending to hit him with the back of my head, but he spun me and tossed me over his shoulder. He sprinted out the door before I could inhale.

I kicked my legs and tried to twist from his grip, but he held tight. Bracing my hands on his back, I raised my head enough to see the vines move and felt a surge of hope. However, they didn't move for Tennen. They stretched for Egrit, who ran toward me, and tangled around her trunk and the trunk of her man. Swiftly came thundering toward us only to be caught in the vines, too. Mr. Crow took flight but was snatched from the air. Despair robbed me of my fight. Why would the beast do this?

In the predawn light, Tennen raced through the open

gates. His shoulder dug into my middle. Nausea rose. Oblivious, or maybe uncaring, he continued on.

We reached the quiet village of Konrall with me on the verge of vomiting. Regardless, as soon as I saw the first house, I opened my mouth to scream, knowing the butcher and the candle maker would come to my aid. Before I could utter a sound, Tennen threw me to the ground and slapped my mouth.

"Not a sound," he warned.

"Piss off!" I cried as I tried to scramble away.

He used his body to pin me and stuffed my mouth with a cloth. Then, holding my arms, he tossed me behind his head and carried me like large game. My breath whooshed out of me for a moment. I still struggled, though. The effort earned me a sharp bite to my inner thigh.

He turned into the alley beside the bakery, and I started to panic. When he kicked his booted foot against the door, I struggled wildly. I tried to use my tongue to push the gag from my mouth as I yelled for help.

"Tennen," the baker cried in delight, eyeing me.

"Bread for life," Tennen demanded harshly.

I understood what he meant to do and thrashed about, hoping he would drop me.

"One loaf a week until the day you die, or one loaf a day for four months."

Tennen nodded just as I managed to wriggle one hand free. I clawed at his face, forgetting the gag in my desperation to be free.

"Inside, quickly," the baker panted.

As soon as the door closed, Tennen swung me from his shoulders and hit me. My ears rang, and I stumbled back, falling against something before crumbling to the ground.

The baker spoke, but I couldn't understand what he said. It sounded as if I had water in my ears, making his words quieter and garbled. I blinked in an attempt to clear my cloudy vision. Tennen's legs passed in front of me. I traced them listlessly to the door. The room spun as the door closed behind him. I struggled to my feet then vomited.

The baker cried in dismay and wrapped a meaty hand around my upper arm to half drag me from the room. I struggled, knowing my pathetic attempts didn't deter him in the least.

He led me through the storefront, where his sister already sat.

"Help." Through my oddly filtered ears, my plea came out slurred.

She looked at me with concern, but the baker waved her aside.

"She..." The water garbled a few of the baker's words. "...to recover."

He opened the door behind the storeroom. It led to a sitting room. He guided me to a lounge and pressed me into the already compressed cushions. I batted his hands away, and he cuffed me upside the head. Not as hard as

M.J. HAAG

Tennen, but he hit the same spot and brought back the nausea.

His hand drifted along the line of my throat, down to the neckline of my pathetically thin nightgown. The palm of his hand skimmed my breast. The touch did not send a familiar tingle to my center, just another rolling wave of nausea. I encouraged revulsion with a forced gag.

The baker jumped back, giving me a moment's reprieve. I brought a hand to my head, rubbing the temple and blinking, trying to clear the fog.

"Let me go," I said.

"I don't think so." His eyes didn't leave my breasts.

I wanted to cry but, instead, looked for a way to escape. The baker used my distraction and pushed me back, pinning me down with his weight.

I couldn't breathe. Panic set in, and I pushed at his shoulders. I barely registered the feel of his hand as he shoved the hem of my nightgown up over my waist. I wore nothing underneath.

I twisted in an effort to move his weight aside enough to draw a decent breath.

The bruising force of his knee parted my legs. Air or not, I would not let him take me. I struggled harder, ignoring the spots that danced in my vision.

The door opened, and I sobbed in relief. But, the baker didn't pause. He began thrusting his hips at me. To my horror, I felt the head of his penis bumping my opening.

However, he was unable to penetrate due to his massive stomach.

"Get off!"

He ignored me and pulled back enough to try to readjust his position. I craned my neck, looking to the door. Tennen, Sara, the smith, and the baker's mother stood there.

"Get him off!"

No one moved. The baker thrust forward again, and his penis came a little closer to my opening. He wiggled one hand under my hip and repositioned me with a grunt.

"Sara!" I screamed.

She looked away, her eyes filled with tears. Tennen smirked. The baker's mother looked deeply troubled, but did not move.

"Help me!"

The baker's mouth moved close to my ear. "Now you are mine."

I turned back toward him, ready to bite his damn nose off. He tilted his hips forward as I opened my mouth with an angry cry. He arched back to avoid me, and the head of his prick bumped to the side, missing my opening completely.

"I will never be yours." I gave up trying to push him away and clawed wildly at his face. My fingernails left a furrow along his cheek.

"Hold her hands," he panted, twisting his head out of the way.

"I think not," a deep voice said from the doorway.

The menacing rumble caused the baker to pause mid-hump. He looked up.

I used the distraction to claw the baker's face savagely. He cried out and tumbled off the lounge, holding his face in pain. I scrambled to my feet, smoothing down my thin gown as if it could protect me. My legs and arms shook.

"She is mine," the baker panted. "You saw us bedding."

"You stunted excuse for a man," I said, turning and kicking him in his soft middle. "I will never be yours."

The baker groaned and curled in on himself.

"You heard the lady," the newcomer said.

I raised my head from the baker to view those who had stood by so callously.

Patrick had pulled Sara to the side. Tennen stood close to them, his hateful expression still on me. I marched right up to him, balled up a fist, and hit him in the mouth. He cried out in shock, and I cradled my hand.

"Bryn was foolish to ever see value in a prick like you," I said, reigning in a sense of calm.

I looked at Sara with condemning eyes but said nothing. Her husband's hand rested on her shoulder. His face remained impassive.

Finally, I looked at the baker's mother, who glanced at her son with a brokenhearted expression. She removed a cloak from the back of a chair, shuffled toward me, and placed it over my shoulders.

While she helped me cover myself, I looked at my

rescuers. The man stood tall. So tall he must have had to duck to fit through the door. His clipped dark hair missed his collar by an inch. His stern brow shadowed his deep blue eyes as his gaze remained on me.

His companion moved slightly, calling my attention. She stood just behind him, her soft hand on his shoulder, much like Patrick's hand on Sara's shoulder. I found that odd, and I ignored her compassionate, soft expression as I focused on her hand. Something seemed so familiar about that hand.

As I stared, my eyes rounded. I looked up at the face. The wrinkles and yellowed teeth were gone but there was no doubt. Rose's face. Aryana's hand.

I looked back at the handsome, stern man, my gaze sweeping him from head to feet. Alec. Liege Lord of the North. The beast had broken the curse.

My heart leapt with joy, until I realized he made no move toward me. I looked at him questioningly, and he grimaced ever so slightly as he met my gaze. Inside, I shattered. I'd known he wouldn't want me after he returned, but I hadn't expected his complete abandonment. My heart broke.

Beaten, nearly raped, and cast aside by the one I loved, I'd suffered enough.

"I want to go home," I whispered, averting my gaze from the pair. "My father's home."

"There is a carriage outside, waiting for you," the Liege Lord said.

He stepped aside, and Aryana/Rose copied his movement. Betrayed by the woman I'd grown to care for more than my own sisters.

Walking stiffly from the room, I left the bakery with my head high. Several people stood in the store's front room. I ignored them all.

Outside, a small, light carriage with a single horse waited; and the driver offered me a hand to step up. I sank into the plush leather seat and blankly stared at the man's coat as he sat in the driver's seat and encouraged the horse into a trot.

I saw little as we left Konrall. The devastation of my world blinded me. I'd lost the beast, the sisters I'd wanted, and the home I'd craved. What was left? I could think of nothing; and in my mind, the baker's weight pressed down on me once more.

THANKS FOR READING DECEIT, Part 2 of the Beastly Tales! I had so much fun writing Benella's life with the beast. Keep reading for an excerpt from Devastation, the conclusion to the Beastly Tales.

AUTHOR'S NOTE

What's with all the cliffhangers?! I know, I know. They can be pretty brutal, but oh-so worth it.

I adored writing this part of Benella's journey with the Beast. So much misunderstanding, danger, and...well, deceit! What did you think of Bryn's little bundle of joy and how she trapped her husband? Or Benella's education at the hands of the Whispering Sisters? There's so much going on in this world it's hard to believe the conclusion is just one book away!

I write because you read. Help me keep writing by encouraging others to read too. The best way to do that (no, don't kidnap friends and force them to read in your basement), is by leaving a review on Goodreads or any of the retailer sites where this title is available. Reviews influence purchases. Purchases are what pay me for all the hours I put into these stories and reimburse me for all the rounds of editing, proofing, and the occasional cover redesigns necessary to keep my books relevant. So, please, leave a review!

Happy reading!

Melissa

SNEAK PEEK OF DEVASATION

Now Available!

The tattered remnants of the world I'd held so dear drifted from my mind. Anger and hate clouded my thoughts.

I shook fiercely but refused to give into the tears that so desperately wanted release. My stomach cramped from the recent abuse and the restraint to contain myself, and my face ached from the blows Tennen and the baker had delivered. Yet, the pain did not distract from the lingering feel of that grotesque, vile man as the carriage rumbled toward the Water. My skin crawled, and my lungs refused to work properly.

I remained so lost in the violent experience that I barely noticed when the carriage pulled before my father's house.

The driver hopped down from his perch and offered a

hand to help me down. I needed the help. The shaking in my legs had only grown worse.

Once I was on my feet, the driver turned to Father's home and knocked on the door. Trembling in Mrs. Mendunge's cloak and my nightgown, I stood behind the man.

Father opened the door, took one look at me, and ushered me in.

"Benella, what's happened?" he said, wrapping an arm around me to steady me.

I could only shake my head. He tried quizzing the driver, but the man bowed and said to expect to hear from his master soon.

That penetrated my clouded mind. My stomach dropped. The returned Lord of the estate. The image of him standing so calmly burned my eyes; still, no moisture gathered.

As soon as the door closed, Father led me to a chair then quickly left to pull water from the well. When he returned, he dipped a cloth into the pail, wrung it out, and held it to my cheek. I flinched from the pain and the reminder of what had happened.

"I'll fetch the physician," he said, already turning away.

"No." I caught his hand to stop him.

I wasn't hurt so badly that I could justify what a physician would cost. I would recover. Yet, as Father faced me with concern, I knew he would insist unless I explained my abused appearance.

I averted my gaze as words spilled forth.

"I interrupted an attempted thievery at the beast's estate," I said, staring at the table. "The beast was...elsewhere. The thief carried me to the baker. The baker attempted to rape me. His grotesque belly saved me," I said in a broken whisper. "I'm shaken and bruised. Nothing that won't heal."

"Oh, my girl." Father knelt beside me and wrapped me in his arms. His compassion almost released the tears I struggled to withhold.

"I don't want to go back," I said in a tight, pained voice. "They all play cruel games. I thought Aryana a friend, but she's the enchantress who has held the beast this whole time. They were both there at the baker's." I lifted my head and met my father's agonized gaze. "Their presence stopped the baker, but they otherwise stood by indifferently."

"I'm so sorry, Bini," my father whispered with tears in his eyes. "I wish I knew how to fix this."

I knew he meant more than the attack I'd suffered. He pulled me back into a comforting hug, trying to protect me as he had from Tennen's bullying when he'd moved us to the Water. Yet, instead of Father making the sacrifice he'd intended, I'd been tricked into staying with the beast who I had thought would protect me as zealously as he'd protected his estate. Sadly, I had wrongly assumed his level of affection for me. The ache in my chest continued to grow but for Father's sake, I withheld my tears.

Father pulled away and offered me the use of his room, along with some of his clothes. After I dressed, I sat on his bed with my elbows on my knees and stared at my folded hands.

All the advice Aryana had given or not given made more sense. She'd used me in her game with the beast. As Rose, she'd dissuaded me, steeling my determination to help. As Aryana, she'd given me the knowledge I'd needed to navigate a world I'd not understood. I recalled all the times she had said she worried about me. She had been sincere; I didn't doubt it. Yet, it hadn't been enough to stop her game.

Finally, tears fell hard and fast.

SERIES READING ORDER

Beastly Tales

Depravity

Deceit

Devastation

Tales of Cinder

Disowned (Prequel)

Defiant

Disdain

Damnation

Resurrection Chronicles

Demon Ember

Demon Flames

Demon Ash

Demon Escape

Demon Deception

Demon Night

More to come!

CPSIA information can be obtained
at www.ICGtesting.com
Printed in the USA
BVHW031510010620
580713BV00001B/244